Zombie Hunter Series Volume 1: Johnny

Chapter 1 – The Neighbor

1.

9:00 AM- This is my first entry in this journal. This is the first time I have written anything since high school. I am 27 years old now. I live in a dilapidated duplex that is owned by my late mothers' friend. I will not use my name or the names of the people in my life for fear that what I write in this journal may one day incriminate me. You see, the reason I am writing in this journal is not to fulfill some childish notion that I am so important that someday one of my distant relatives or perhaps one of my children or grandchildren are going to read this in hopes of getting to know me, their hero. That is laughable! To even think of the idea of having children, let alone a girlfriend or something resembling such a thing would lead to nothing but disappointment. I've no time for that. Instead, I am going to use this as a scientist who uses an instrument to better understand the things that I think, dream, feel, and of course, the things I do.

2.

3:00 AM- I awoke violently this morning. I am drenched in sweat like I was running a marathon. My mind is racing. I had the dream again. I appear to be very young, and I am running around my grandparents’ house. I walk past the dining room where my mother and her new husband are fighting when all of a sudden, he picks up a kitchen knife off of the table and slashes her throat. As she goes into shock from the injury, she looks at me and smiles. That is always the point where I wake up. My head hurts like it does when you drink something cold too fast. Oh, and to make matters worse, I am out of my medication for not only my god-awful migraines, but also for my other problems. You see, the doctors all think I have schizophrenia. This is because I told them that the voice of my dead friend talks to me and tells me to do things. They give me this medicine, and everything is supposed to just “go away”. Well, it doesn’t. I still hear his voice loud and clear, and I still see him just fine. However, without it, I can no longer pretend to be normal. I get depressed and I cannot function correctly. I cannot bear the thought of going out into the world and dealing with the public, which usually leads to some outburst or public scene which of course is why I am unemployed right now.

Unfortunately, I cannot get any more medication until I see my shrink so until then, I have to do as my she tells me and “tough it out”. On the bright side, my mother’s old friend is kind enough not to kick me out of this place even though I have not paid rent in at least three months. The utilities are covered in the rent not that it matters. But if it weren’t for him, I would not have a place to stay. I also wouldn’t have a place to hide when I need to esca pe and hide from the world when I need to. Well, I think I will try once again to go back to sleep. So, I guess this is good night for now.

3.

8:00 AM- Well, good news! Not really, but I digress. I have a new upstairs neighbor. She has two young children who introduced themselves while she was moving her stuff into the place. I was out checking my mail in hopes that I would get some piece of mail other than the usual bills that I ignore seeing as how I don't make money. Her son informed me that I looked like a hobo. How fucking adorable. He then went on to tell me that they moved away from their daddy because he went to live with their mommy's ex friend. I told him it was probably because he was an ugly kid, and his mom was equally ugly. I'm not trying to befriend these people. They are loud, annoying, and most of all, they have no sense of privacy. I found that I now have to lock my door since the daughter who is I think nine or ten, seems to think this whole house belongs to them and she doesn't need to stay out of my personal space. The girl didn't knock on the door or anything. She just barged right on in! Their mom is no better than the kids. She screams at them all day until the babysitter shows up, and then it's off to work. From the way she is dressed when she leaves; I think she is some kind of stripper or something equally shitty

. I can see this is going to end well. She has been here one day, and I am already sick of her shit. I need to think of a way to get r id of this family fast.

4.

2:00 AM- I can't seem to get more than an hour of sleep at a tim e. My neighbor upstairs is having sex with what I assume is a hu mpback whale judging by the plaster from the ceiling that hit me in the face. That, and of course the horrifyingly loud moans he is making. She sounds like she is just going through the motions u ntil he finally climbs his sweaty, disgusting, fat body off of her. I may have been wrong about the stripper thing. She may be a pr ostitute. An hour goes by and finally a little peace and quiet. I gu ess this means I can go back to sleep. So, goodnight, I guess.

3:00 AM- Never mind! I guess the quiet thing decided to take the night off. The mother upstairs is now engaged in an all-out screa m fest upstairs with what I am assuming is her client. I guess he didn't know that his little excursion with her was a paid visit, and she expected the money right away. I had fallen asleep at about 2:10 so I didn't hear the beginning of this annoyance. What I do know is that I woke up to one of them throwing something, and t hen her screaming at him "WHAT DO YOU MEANYOU DON'T HAVE THAT KIND OF FUCKING MONEY!?!?!" I guess I was rig ht about her being a prostitute.

9:00 AM- I have decided that I may make the most of my day. I didn't get too much sleep, but I feel pretty good today. I think I will go to the park for a while and maybe even look for a job. Wish me luck! Oh wait. This is a journal. I forgot I am essentially talking to myself. Whatever! I am going out and looking for a job.

6:00 PM- Well, that didn't go at all the way I had hoped it would. All this little adventure out of the house without my medication has proven to me that I should not face the public without it. I went to the park like I had mentioned earlier. I was there for about two hours before some asshole police officer told me that some of the mothers thought they saw me “eyeing” their kids. Yeah, because a man can't sit on a park bench, wearing sunglasses, facing the playground, and not be a fucking pervert! I am not a fucking pervert! Of course, I reacted pretty much that way. I caused a big scene, and the cops physically kicked me out of the park. The officers called me a “Fucking Bum” and proceeded to lecture me all the way to the station about not over-reacting and cussing in front of children. You know, because those people at the park acted so rationally. Of course, I spent four hours sitting in a room where the cops interrogated me like they wanted me to confess to being a sick pervert and admit I need help. They even used the old “Good Cop, Bad Cop” routine they use in all of those stupid cop drama shows from TV. After all that shit, they produced a written statement from my shrink who is apparently on vacation. The statement said “________ is a very disturbed individual who is in need of medication in order to function properly in society. He is prone to fits of narcissistic rage, depression, suicidal behavior, and psychotic outbursts. My client, however, is not a sexual deviant. As a matter of fact I do not believe my client to be or ever to have been sexually aroused by anything at all. I will be sending an expedited prescription for his medication which will arrive at the station later this afternoon. Please observe him taking his medications as prescribed, give him the rest to take with him, and send him home approximately one hour later. This will give the medicine long enough to start working. Thank you very much for your patience and cooperation.” About 4 PM according to the clock in the holding cell, the asshole officer that arrested me comes up and tells me to take the medicine he is holding in his I assume, unwashed, and sweaty palm. I take the medication while trying not to think about him taking a piss and getting some on his hands while he is pulling up his zipper just mere minutes before taking the pills out of the bottle and giving them to me. The pills have the flavor of sweat or piss, maybe both, which doesn’t help the situation at all. I try not to gag while he takes an extra-longtime getting my water from the cooler behind him. After I take the pills, I am forced to sit here for another hour and a half. At this point I am escorted out of the station, given a new, full prescription of my medication, and told by that asshole officer to “Stay out of trouble.” Fuck you! I think to myself. At least one goo d thing came from my adventure. I got my meds. Now I can function properly as my shrink said in that ever so flattering letter to the police. Thanks, I guess.

5.

3:33 AM- The voice is loud in my head tonight. I try to sleep, but it nags and nags at me until I am forced to do what he wants me to do. Like I had said previously, the medication helps me deal with   my other problems, but does nothing to stop the sound of my friends' whispery, metallic voice telling me to do inexplicably horrible things. "That woman upstairs is a whore, and she should be punished for the way she is!" It's hard sometimes to tell whether it is real or if I am just having "Audio-Hallucinations" as my shrink likes to call them. Tonight, the punishment he speaks of is to hide in her car until she gets in to go to work. That gives me about a half an hour to do what needs to be done and get back to my house before she is expected to be at work, and someone starts wondering where she is. The method of execution tonight is to be suffocation. I will don my favorite attire tonight. A tight fitting black thermal shirt tucked into my properly fitting, not too tight, but not too loose cargo pants with the Velcro pocket fasteners so that I won't lose any buttons in the vehicle thus leaving some sort of evidence. I have shaved my head, eyebrows, and face clean of any hair and have also made sure to wear surgical gloves and have a hot shower with no soap so as to leave no DNA or distinct smell behind. I used an abrasive showering gel with an abrasive scrubbing tool, like the women use these days “It’s all about exfoliating the dead skin away from the body in order to expose that younger, healthier, radiant skin!” the ladies at the bath store in the mall would tell me. Also good for making sure you don’t leave any dead skin particles behind at the crime scene. My nails have been cut so as not to leave scratches indicating that the suspect may have any dead skin or anything of the sort caught under their fingernails. I realize that these precautions may seem a little extreme, but let’s face it; I don’t think being caught is going to work out for me. I am not a person who is considered to be small per say, but I’m definitely not what would be considered an imposing force of nature. I am a rather non-threatening presence which is what makes what I do that much easier to do without being suspected. Aside from the little stint at the station yesterday, the cops don’t know who I am. And of course, I have my shrink to back me up. But given the events that took place and what was said in that letter, the cops may actually think of me as a suspect. Unfortunately, that is irrelevant to my friend. “What needs to be done needs to be done and cannot be compromised”.

8:45 PM- I am having second thoughts about what is going to transpire in the next 45 minutes. I am having serious anxiety; my palms are sweating in their latex gloves, my breathing is heavy, and my heartbeat is erratic. But there is no turning back now. My friend will have his way tonight. He tells me to take another one of the pills my shrink gave me so it will ease the tension. I do a s I am told. Wish me luck.

6.

02:00 AM- Well, that didn't turn out the way I had assumed it was going to. I got in the car as I had planned to. I laid in the car waiting until she got in and she started to drive. She had then got on the phone with who I assumed at the time was her mother. She was very upset with the way her life was and was struggling to take care of her kids. She recounted the experience she had with the whale-like person she had over the other night. Apparently, he had the wrong idea about what the arrangement was. He was unaware that women didn't find people like him at all attractive and won't just walk up to him asking if he wants to have a little fun for free. She was crying and telling her mom she was sorry for being such a disappointment to her. Her mother was outright insulting her, telling her she was a horrible mother, a failure as a daughter, and most of all a sick, disgusting whore. Despite my friend telling me I would be doing her a favor by extinguishing her life, I couldn't bring myself to do it. I'm not really sure as to what was really stopping me seeing as how I have never had this happen before. I never understood the concept of not doing what you set out to do. Maybe was the whole not shitting where you sleep thing. I mean, if I kill her, it will bring the cops right to my doorstep at some point. Then all they have to do is put two and two together and they will figure out It's me. So, I guess my neighbor will remain unharmed. I guess this means no peace for m

e. My friend will soon express his displeasure of the situation. For now, he is strangely quiet. I guess I will take advantage of that fact and get some sleep.

4:00 AM- I can't sleep. My head is killing me, and my shrink did not prescribe me my medication for the migraines. My friend has been screaming at me in disapproval for the act of mercy I showed. He tells me that I am a failure, and I will not get any peace until he is satisfied. I have taken more of the medication than was prescribed in an attempt to get some sort of silence out of him. He does not relent. "YOU CANNOT GO BACK ON OUR AGREEMENT! NOT AFTER WHAT YOU DID TO ME! NOW GO OUT THERE AND DON'T COME BACK UNTIL YOU HAVE SATISFIED MY DEMANDS!" He keeps at it until I tell him what he wants to hear. He demands a blood sacrifice, and I must obey.

But not this morning. My head is feeling ten times too large with writhing, unbearable pain.

I must rest. Finally, at about 5:00 AM, he subsides but warns that he will not be so kind tonight if I don't do what we agreed upon.

Chapter 2 – Blood Sacrifice

7.

9:00 AM- I have found my sacrifice. After I woke up yesterday at about noon, I'm not really too sure what time it was, but some time close to noon, I decided to get dressed, and go out looking for work. Based off of the last time I went to the park, I decided I would probably want to stay away from there for a while. Besides, if I have to put up with the looks those women will give me and pretend not to notice them talking to each other and watch one of them mouth the word "pervert" one more time, I may actually go give them a real reason to call the cops. I can picture the reaction of the local people in this town, they would all gather outside of the jail and demand I be killed in front of the whole town like this was the wild west. I am unfortunate that I am in a town full of pretty much the bottom of the barrel society. I am honestly surprised that we have franchised fast food restaurants and a school. I'm surprised that any of these inbred yokels can actually read. Of course, someone is going to do the inevitable and tell me that god is going to punish me and send me to hell to burn forever in the lake of fire or some other equally asinine statement. Let's get things straight before I move on with what happened. I feel I should clarify this. Look, I know I have no heaven waiting for me when I die, but It's not like I think I'm going to hell either. As a matter of fact, let it be known that I don't believe in the bible, god, the devil, or in religion in general. To me, I don't find it easy to believe there are good or evil people in this world. Just people who do things and people who don't. If god existed, then not one per son would fit into his or her divine plan. Thousands of people, w omen, children, and even the elderly have been slaughtered in t he name of a god that was created by humans in order to explai n the un-explainable. Why are we here? Where did we come fro m? Blah, blah, blah! You're fucking kidding me, right? If you hav e an urge to kill people, to rape children, to steal, to give into lust and commit adultery, smoke, swear, covet your neighbors' spou se, etc. and the only thing stopping you is fear of what god is goi ng to do to you? Well, I have news for you! You are just as evil a s the person who actually does it. You are just as guilty of it. The re is no such thing as good people, there are just cowards. At le ast I don't deny what I am. Either way, I am babbling, so, let me continue on with my finding of a proper sacrifice. I am trying to t urn a new leaf of sorts. I will kill only those that I am sure nobod y is going to care to miss. This isn't really because I am trying to be a hero or anything, but more because I am less likely to g et caught. The cops will only go through the motions of finding a dirt bag child molesters' killer, but that's all they will do. Just eno ugh to calm down the liberal media.

I was taking a break from my job search at a local fast-food plac e. I bought a cheeseburger and a small fry from the "value" meal . I asked for an ice water, they charged me an extra 50 cent s fo r a cup that costs maybe 10 cents at the most, ice, which is mad e from water, and of course the water itself is supposed to be fre e seeing as how it is just tap water that goes through a suppose d filter, and while we're on the subject of "value", if it is such a va lue, why is it that the salad is ten times more expensive? I would rather eat a salad then a “value” cheeseburger and fry, but since the salad costs more than the burger, fries, and water combined , then I guess it’s the “value” for me. Never mind. I was trying to enjoy the shitty meal I was eating when, from across the restaur ant, there stood my next “victim”. I don’t really like to call people like him victims because they tend to do something that makes it easy for me to do what it is that I do. It is almost as if he were pu t there just for me to see and to exact punishment upon. I love th ese kinds of people. There’s never a second thought as to whet her I will feel any remorse for doing it. I don’t believe him to be a victim of anything but his own doing. Either way, my supposed vi ctim was standing with what seemed to be his wife and her daug hter. He was a rather tall person, wearing what looked like a cro ss between a biker and a gang member. He wore a blue bandan a covering his greasy, blonde, shoulder length hair. He was wea ring a sleeveless leather jacket over a plaid lumberjack type shir t which was stained with sweat and dirt, his face and his hands l ooked coarse and worn as if he worked construction from the ag e of five, his arms looked like he had worked out a bit. From the looks of him and the way he carries himself, he may have been i n prison before. Anyways, he was standing with the wife and her daughter, who seemed to be about twelve or so years old. I coul d tell she wasn’t his daughter based off of complexion, eye color , and facial structure. You know someone’s daughter when you compare them to the parent. She looked as if she was terrified o f him. I could tell why. Every time his wife wasn’t paying attentio n, he would look menacingly at her. He would make sexual gestures, lick his lips, and wiggle his tongue at her. I watched this just as the rest of the cowards did. Nobody said anything to him or to his wife about it. As if it wasn't happening right in front of them. My friend whispered into my ear as if to make sure no-one else heard him, "He is the one I want. Kill him for me, will you?" "I will "I tell him. But first, I need to understand him, know where he works, where he lives, where he goes, and of course, his habits and routes. No. this won't be sloppy work like the ill-conceived idea I had in plan for my neighbor. This will be precise, and vengeful. I stole some kid's bike from the stand outside of the restaurant. My intuition was correct when I was trying to figure out which vehicle was his, it was a green, beat down pickup truck, riddled with rust holes, caked with dried mud, and of course the tires were taller than me. On the back bumper there was a sticker, "Discourage inbreeding ban country music". Ironic I thought, given the situation. Nonetheless, I followed them through town. At times they went so fast that I had to pedal to the point of exhaustion just to keep them in view. Thankfully, there are a lot of stop-lights in this town. People complain about that fact, I guess they never had to follow someone all the way through town on a kid's ten speed bike before. After what seemed like at least an hour, he stopped in front of a local coffee shop. He then kissed the wife goodbye and she stepped out wearing her waitress outfit. It was the same kind of uniform I would see them wearing in all those movies where there is a diner scene. It took long enough for me to at least catch my breath. My throat was dry and I was sweating prof

usely. I unfortunately had no time to stop and get a drink, so I lic
ked the sweat from my upper lip so I would at least get a little m
oisture in my mouth making it a little easier to swallow. After a c
ouple minutes, he was off again. I followed for another 15 minut
es to a quaint neighborhood consisting mostly of trailers. There
were a couple of small houses, mostly with lots of abandoned ch
ildren's toys and cars up on blocks. They pulled into the drivewa
y of an off-white doublewide trailer. The lawn was poorly kept. T
here were brown patches of bare dirt that took up most of the ya
rd, the rest was covered with brown, dried grass patches that lo
oked like they could catch fire just from the thought of a spark b
eing near them. The windows had those old plastic sun-shields
on them. They were sun-bleached and brittle. I watching him op
en the door to the trailer, I noticed he didn't use a key to unlock t
he door. Assuming by the time they dropped the wife off, I guess
ed she would be there for at least 8 hours before they went back
out to pick her up from work. Since the sun was up, I didn't want
to go sneaking around quite at that moment. There was a playgr
ound about a hundred yards away with a perfect view of their ho
me. I went over to the park and waited for the sun to go down.

When it got dark, I abandoned the bike in some bushes so I coul
d get to it fast if need be. I snuck through the woods behind their
side of the neighborhood. I assumed that if people saw me cree
ping around the neighborhood where I was obviously not from, t
hat may raise enough suspicion for them to recall seeing me da
ys before the gruesome murder of one of their neighbor. So I did

it quietly and stealthily. I crept up to the back of the house. Standing there, I heard a muffled scream and some grunting coming from the bedroom area. I went over to the window of the room the sound seemed to be coming from. When I looked into the window to see what was happening, I could see both of them. He had her hands tied behind her back using what looked like a pink scarf, her mouth was gagged with the greasy bandana he was wearing in the restaurant, and she was face down on the bed. I could see her face in the mirror in front of her. She was red faced and crying through the bandana. He was making her watch. She would try to fight him off, but when she did, he would just pull up on her bound hands far enough to cause pain. She would then subside and let him do what he wanted. He was sweating and breathing heavily. When he finally finished, he grabbed her oversized stuffed bear and used it to wipe off. He then threw the bear at her. She didn't respond, instead, she just laid there staring emotionlessly into the mirror. He left the room and closed the door.

I snuck over to the kitchen window. He grabbed a beer from the fridge, sat down on the couch, and turned on the television. He was watching Jeopardy. He sat there for a couple of minutes when he yelled at the top of his lungs, "GET YOUR LAZY ASS IN THE FUCKIN' SHOWER, AND HURRY THE FUCK UP! WE GOTTA PICK YOUR MOM UP SOON! DON'T MAKE ME COME BACK THERE GOD DAMMIT!" I watched as they left. Again, they didn't lock the door. As they pulled out of the driveway, I could se e the expression on her face, it was cold and unresponsive.

When they were out of sight, I went into the house. I looked around the living room for a minute when I spotted a paycheck stub on the coffee table. It had the name of the construction company he worked on the envelope. There also was a letter from the friend of the court. Our friend was a paroled ex-convict. In the letter it read that he had an appointment a few days from now, this was for his monthly visit with his parole officer. I guess I'm going to have to wait until after then to deal with him. I walked into the daughter's bedroom and grabbed the pink scarf from under her bed and left. I picked up the bike I had stolen and pedaled back to the same restaurant I stole it from. I placed it back where I got it. I'm not that kind of person. I may be a monster, but I am no thief, unless you count the scarf. I am planning on using it for something, so it will be a necessary evil for now. Fortunately, it was late enough when I returned the bike that the restaurant was closed. So, all that being said, I have three days counting the remainder of this day, to go out and look for work before I have to deal with our soon to be deceased child rapist douche bag. As a leaving remark before you judge me for not taking action while he was committing the act, it is that action, which has sealed the deal for me. I do not think this was the first time he has done this to her, but, if I can help it, this will be the last. I am what I am, but I could never do that to a child. Killing is one thing, but how can someone be turned on by a child. That's just fucking sick.

5:00 PM- Well, some good news! I have a job interview at the lo
cal crematorium. The person I turned in the application with ask
ed me a few questions like my preference of schedule, if I was u
ncomfortable with being around dead bodies, being alone with t
hem at night without supervision, things like that. I told him what
he wanted to hear which was that I would have no problems wit
h any of those things. I actually preferred to work alone and that
I require no supervision. So, tomorrow at 9:00 AM I have the int
erview.

7.

4:00 AM- I had the dream again. This time, when I watched my
mother smile at me while she bled from her jugular, I looked at
my stepfathers face. Instead of seeing his face, I see my own. H
e smiled right before slashing his own throat. Something that sh
ould be clarified is that this was not the defining moment that ma
de me the way I am. By the time I was that age, I had already kil
led someone. I used to kill small animals and torture insects. I gr
aduated to humans at the age of nine. My best friend and I were
playing in the woods behind my house. My mother was unaware
he was out there as were his parents. I wanted to show him my
collection of dead animals. The problem was his reaction to the
pile of dead, mutilated animal carcasses. He was very upset and
disturbed by what he saw. He then tried to run and said he was

going to tell my mom. So I took the knife that I stole from mom's kitchen, and I drove it into the lower part of his back. I pulled the knife out just as fast as I stuck it into him. When I pulled the blad e out, there was nothing at first, and then there was blood. Ther e was so much blood! He started screaming, so I tackled him an d put my hand over his mouth and nose. I was just trying to get him to stop screaming at first, but he started to struggle and try t o fight me off, so I stabbed him in the chest, and I kept stabbing him. Even after he stopped moving, and it was more than appar ent that he had passed, I kept stabbing him for what seemed lik e an eternity. It being the woods, I decided the best thing to do i s to get the body somewhere near the river and wait for the wolv es to come. At this point at least it would look like he was maule d by wild animals, eaten and left for dead. I positioned his body against a tree near the river, and waited. Eventually I decided it would be a good idea to climb a tree to keep from attention bein g drawn to me. I waited until the sun started to go down. The wo lves finally came and I watched as they devoured my dead frien d. I never felt bad for what I did. I actually didn't feel anything fro m the time he died. I wasn't even really able to show any kind of emotion about my friend's untimely demise when I got home an d told my mom that my friend and I had been playing out by the river and we were attacked by wolves. I was covered in blood, di rt, and other crap I could find near the gruesome scene. I cut my self to make it look like one of the wolves got a swipe on me as well, and made up the lie that I escaped up a tree but my friend wasn't so fortunate. I told her and the local police that I had to w atch helplessly as he screamed for help while the wolves tore him apart and ate him alive. I described the wolves fighting over what little was left of my dear friend. Everyone bought the story but my stepdad. They constantly fought over it for another year. That and my mother had apparently a bad habit of smoking pot with the neighborhood teenagers who she had often cheated on him with. I was not all that surprised at the moment of my mother's death. Nor was I all that shocked about my step father's death. As a matter of fact, I think I was the only one in the family that was unable to show any emotions or shock over the whole thing. My grandparents always told me up until this happened that I was their “special little man” and that they would always be there for me. A week later, after I stayed at their house with them, I over heard my grandparents talking about me. They had assumed I was in the living room watching cartoons. I was thirsty so I was going to ask for a drink of water. My grandfather told my grandmother, “There is something wrong with that kid. I'm telling you something isn't right with him. That little kid gives me the fucking creeps. He doesn't seem affected at all by his parents' deaths he wasn't affected when he watched his friend being eaten by wolves, what in the fuck is wrong with him?” My grandmother did nothing but nod her head in agreement. He then said “I'm going to call social services and have them come and get him. Maybe they can handle him, but I can't, and neither will you. If anyone asks us, we will say he is out of control and violent. Maybe they'll give him counseling. But we can't do that for him. It is his fault that they ended up this way, and I don't want him fucking our lives up too. We are far too old to raise another kid, let alone a fucked up little kid like him. Can you imagine what he will be like as a te enager? Shit, as a matter of fact, after he leaves, I think it woul d be in our better interest to never speak of, or to him again. He won't exist to us anymore." Grandma again, did nothing but nod in agreement.

It was when I got to the group home that things changed for me. I was seeing a shrink. She made the determination, after recordi ng my reaction to images of ink blots and talking to me about my experiences with death, that I should be medicated. It was soon after I started taking the medication, that I started having these v isits from my old friend.

10:00 AM- I went to my job interview at the crematorium at 9:00 this morning. They asked me the same set of questions that the y had asked before. I gave them all the same answers. Needles s to say, I got the job. This will work out great for me. My schedu le is Monday thru Friday, 9PM to 6AM with an hour lunch break i n the middle. The fact that all I need to do is clock in at 9 and clo ck out at 6, I have no supervisor until 5:30, there are no camera s, and no people around to verify my coming and going. This will make my life so much less complicated. On top of that, if I figure out the timing and procedures, I could use this place to dispose of bodies. All this time, I have been killing outside of the county, hitch-hiking, finding a victim, and leaving them in the woods for t he animals to eat. Now, I have a way of getting rid of the bodies without a trace of evidence. The reason I am worried about timin g is because I need to find out how long it takes to cremate the body, and how long it will take to cool the oven off enough to wh ere I can safely clean it, and also have it fully cooled before the supervisor gets in for work. It may seem a bit odd to them that th e oven is still warm after being off all night. Just a thought. I plan on taking care of business at some point tomorrow night, so I gu ess I will use the internet to research some of the procedures an d whatnot.

According to the search I did, it can take on an average of 2 to 2 ½ hours for the body to be cremated. After that is done, the bod y must then be run through a processor in order to be broken do wn into the desired dust state. Altogether, then entire process sh ould take about 3 hours. Since the oven runs between 1600 and 1800 degrees, I will need to do this fairly early in the evening. T onight is my first night working the new job, so that will also give me a better feel of what is going to transpire. Meanwhile, I need to go take care of some errands and get myself ready for work.

8:30 PM- I am getting ready to leave for work. I bought everythin g my boss wrote down on a list for me. Non-slip work boots, lon g sleeve work shirt, kaki work pants, a pair of protective glasses, and of course, an apron. The crematorium is supposed to suppl y the rest. I am off to work now.

Wish me luck!

8.

6:35 AM- Well, the first night went very well. I learned all of the c
leaning procedures needed to clean the ovens and the processo
rs. It turns out that in order to clean the ovens, I need to run the
m for an hour before letting them cool for another hour, and then
I can wipe them down. Also, strangely enough, they needed so
meone to run the machines at night and asked if I would be inter
ested in making a little more money and learn how to do that as
well. So, I am starting to think that this is going to work out grea
t. I am not only going to be able to dispose of the bodies without
being found out, but I will also be able to clean up the mess and
not be suspected of any wrong doing when the ovens are still w
arm the next morning. Unfortunately, I am going to have to go ta
ke care of my soon to be deceased friend before my shift starts.
I will have to put the body somewhere close to the crematorium
so I can get my work done, and also dispose of him within the ti
meframe needed. So, I am going to go ahead and get some sle
ep, prepare, and then go perform the sacrifice.

4:00 PM- I am going to go take care of my friend. He should be done with his appointment with the parole officer and back at the trailer by now. Hopefully, his step-daughter isn't there. Not sure what I am going to do with her if she is. I normally have no probl em killing witnesses, but I would rather not do it if possible. It al ways makes things far more complicated than they need to be. Unfortunately, since it is daylight right now, this is going to be far more risky. I don't have the freedom of being able to do all of thi s under the cover of night so I will need to be extra cautious. I h ave packed in my bag the following items: two rolls of duct tape, a straight razor, a couple sheets of 20 grit sandpaper, a plunger handle, some heavy duty trash bags, latex gloves, and of course , the pink scarf that I had taken from his house. This is going to be a very special night for him, and for my friend who has been patiently waiting for this. He has been strangely quiet. I think this is because he knows it is going to happen. I am not backing out of this one. This person, this "victim" needs to die tonight.

8:00 PM- The deed has been done. It went better than I had tho ught it would. I went to his neighborhood on foot. I walked into th e woods behind the place again. I made sure nobody saw me of

course. And as I crept up to his place, the daughter stormed out
the front door and got in the truck. She then peeled out of the dri
veway. She looked halfway panicked and also looked like she h
ad been in a fight. Her hair was a mess, her makeup was smear
ed in smoky streaks down her face, and she also had what look
ed like spattered blood on her face and clothes. Not a lot, but en
ough to suggest she was on the winning end of the fight. My gue
ss was it was with our buddy. Maybe she took care of him for m
e. I thought to myself. So, when she was out of sight, I snuck int
o the house. The living room was trashed along with the rest of t
he place. There was a broken forty ounce bottle of beer in the m
iddle of the living room. The coffee table was smashed into splin
ters and there was blood smeared on the walls going down the
hallway. I could hear some groaning, shuffling, and labored brea
thing coming from what seemed to be her room. I snuck as quiet
ly as I could so as not to be noticed. When I looked in her room,
he was sitting on the ground, slumped over a bit, leaned against
her bed. His face was lacerated and he seemed to be suffering f
rom a concussion. Her room and the living room both reeked of
beer. My guess is that he got rough with her again, she got fed u
p, and somehow got his beer away from him and smashed him
over the head. I walked into the room, and stood over him, study
ing him for a moment. My friend was in my ear telling me how h
appy he was that we were going through with it. I ignored him as
my curiosity took hold. "What happened? Did she get tired of yo
u raping her? I mean, that's the only reason I can think of that w
ould leave you in the state you're in right now. How, did she do t

his to you? She is what? Twelve years old? You look maybe ab out forty? That shit is just fucking hilarious!" I said to him mockin gly. He looked up at me as if not surprised I was here. "Are you going to get me out of here?" he asked. The desperation in his v oice told me he was too far in shock to care or even think as to whom I was and why I was there. "Yeah, I'm here to get you out of here" I said. So I helped him to his feet. We barely got into the cover of the woods when the daughter and her mother pulled up in the truck. She must have went straight to where her mother w as working and told her what happened due to the looks on both of their faces. We hid in the bushes until they went into the hous e. He looked at me terrified and said "they will kill me if we don't find somewhere to hide for a minute." I said nothing. "The trailer a couple houses down is abandoned and we could hide there fo r a minute at least till they leave." I nodded and helped him to hi s feet. Just as he had said, the trailer was dark. The sun was on its way down, so I figured I might as well get this over with as so on as possible. I had to jimmy the door a bit to get it open. We g ot into the place and the smell was horrendous. It smelled like ol d, dead things. All of the windows were boarded shut. The carpe t was deteriorated in places bad enough to where the wooden fl oor was exposed. In the middle of the dimly lit living room, there was a coffee table that was caked thick with dust and dead bugs . He was resting against the wall close to the hallway. I walked i nto the kitchen to see if that was where the smell was coming fr om. In the sink, there were dishes that must have been in there f or years. The water still ran, but it was brown and smelled like ro tten eggs. I didn't dare to open the refrigerator seeing as how the rest of the house was in such great shape. By this time, he had made his way to the bathroom. This whole time, I had been carrying my bag. It was getting very heavy so I decided to put it down for a second. As I passed the bathroom, I looked in. He was looking at himself in the mirror. "That bitch! I can't believe she did that to me!" I asked him what happened. "She is a little fucking cunt and her mother doesn't discipline her enough. So I had to do it. She was getting all fuckin' smart mouthed and I had to fix that shit for her. She grabbed my beer outta my hand and hit me with it! I'm gonna go back over there to straighten her out later tonight!" I nodded. I assumed by this time, he figured I was on his side. I went back out to the living room and grabbed my bag. I pulled out the pink scarf from the bag and stuck it into my pocket. He stumbled out of the bathroom and walked past me to the kitchen. He started looking for something in the drawers. I crept up behind him as he was mumbling something to himself and I took the scarf out of my pocket. I then put it around his neck from behind, tightened it, and started walking backwards making sure to keep him off balance. He struggled to get to his feet for a moment, and then, he slumped, limp, to the ground. I dragged his body over to the coffee table and began duct taping him face down on the coffee table. I pulled his pants and underwear down and then taped his legs so they were open and he could not pull free. It took a whole roll to tape him down and of course tape his mouth so he couldn't scream too loud. I went into the back bedroom where I had spotted an old standup mirror. I placed the mirror in

front of him so he could see what was happening behind him. I
put on my latex gloves and retrieved the plunger handle, the san
d paper, and the other roll of duct tape out of the bag. I first put t
he tape with the sticky side up onto the handle. I then wrapped it
with the sand paper and reinforced it with more duct tape. He st
arted to wake up when I had finished the sand paper toy I made
for him. He looked terrified and confused. I walked around to wh
ere he could see me clearly. I then went on to tell him how I had
watched him do what he did to her and how I had been planning
on doing this. I let him know what I had planned on doing to h
im. I showed him the plunger handle and also laid out the scarf,
the razor, and the sandpaper. He started screaming through his
nose. I went over again where he could see me. “Have some f
ucking dignity!” I told him. I then went back behind him and told
him to look in the mirror. As soon as he looked up at me, I shove
d the plunger into his ass. He screamed and blood instantly start
ed pouring out. With every scream, I would shove it in harder an
d deeper. He started to lose consciousness so I would stop and
slap him in the face to wake him back up. He screamed what so
unded like “I’m sorry”, through the tape, but I couldn’t really be s
ure what was being said. I wasn’t about to remove it so he could
speak clearly either. As a finale’, I made sure he was awake, ca
strated him, and let him bleed out. After the bleeding stopped, I
knew I needed to get him out of there and get cleaned up for wo
rk. Not to mention I needed to put him somewhere I could e
asily retrieve him to bring him to the ovens. So, I wrapped him in
a blanket, and dragged him out of the house and into the woods.

I stole a nearby car and threw him in the trunk. Once I drove around for a bit, I spotted a seemingly abandoned gas station. After determining it was a good place, being close enough to my work for me to walk over to on my break, not to mention there seemed to be a much needed lack of people in the area and lots of darkness, I dumped his body in a ditch behind the building. After making sure I couldn't clearly spot him from just walking by, I left him there for later. I am going to go ahead and get ready for work. Hopefully all ends well and I will be making another entry in the morning.

9.

7:00 AM- Well, I did it. I walked onto my shift, cleaned up all of the necessary areas before my lunch break, snuck over to where his body was, and got him into the building. I had removed all of his jewelry and also had to pull a gold tooth he had. Other than that, I had no problems getting him in the oven, processed him, and put his remains in a shoe box. I then sealed the box and placed it in my backpack. I cleaned all of the ovens above and beyond the standards. When my boss came in to do his normal spot-check before I left for the day, he was nothing but compliments. “I knew it was a great idea to have you work here. That’s why I picked you, there just seemed to be something about you that screamed you were right for the job.” I thought to myself “that’s funny! I was thinking the same thing when I applied.” Now, with the blood sacrifice being done, my friend should be satisfied for a bit. He always goes quiet for a while afterwards.

9:00 PM- I was awakened again by my friend. “That was an awesome show buddy!” He exclaimed with a disturbing amount of enthusiasm. “You keep doin’ it like that and we could be doing this till the day that you die! Not me of course, I’m already dead and well, you’ll be sooner or later… Unless this is like that movie where the killer started haunting people’s dreams, then that would be pretty goddamned fun if you ask me!” Ugh! What do you wan t now man?! I asked him. I have a splitting headache and you are not helping at all. “I just wanted to congratulate you is all buddy! I haven’t seen you do anything that gruesome since well, me!” I got up and took my medication. I was hoping it might at least calm down the amount of paranoia I had over my newly found method of disposal. What if I left a tooth, a fingernail, or any evidence at all? This was the first time I went outside of my tried and true method. So of course I am feeling a bit of the jitters as to what could happen. Either way, I am falling away from the story at hand. My friend went on and on for what seemed like a half an hour before he finally came to the conclusion that we need to do this more often and on a grander scale. I asked him what exactly he had in mind. He went on to tell me that the neighbor has all types of dirt bags come to her house all the time and I would be intelligent to take advantage of that fact. I mean, it’s not like they are going to call their wives and let them know that they’re going over to some whore’s house to fuck them after spending half their paycheck on lap dances at the strip club no are they? I think not. So this, to me, sounded like a good idea. I will have to implement this plan right away.

I just got home from another night of work. I didn’t kill anyone of
course tonight. I won’t be doing this every night. The stress woul
d kill me on its own. I did however pay close attention to the new
s. Not one word about the ex-con I killed the other night. My gue
ss at the time was that the daughter and mother were still not all
that sure what had happened. So of course in that assumption, t
hey probably aren’t going to say anything. They’re just happy he
’s gone. I think I will go check out the scene and see if there has
been any activity I should be worried about. I will go before I hav
e to be at work. Until then, I’m going to go ahead and get some
sleep.

7:30 PM- After I woke up from a good days sleep, I went for a w
alk. I walked all the way to where my latest victim had lived. Loo
king around the neighborhood, it was as if nothing horrible had h
appened and not one person seemed like they were even a little
suspicious. This has to be the weirdest feeling I have ever had. I
completely erased someone from existence and no one seemed
to miss him at all. I think I made a great decision when I chose t
o just kill people that wouldn’t be missed. I snooped around the t
railer where they had lived. The mom and daughter were both th
ere. It must have been her day off from the diner or something.
Either way I peeked into each room that I could and everything l
ooked clean and organized. It was as if getting rid of this animal
that lived in there had completed reversed their quality of life for
the better. I almost felt like a super hero, but of course my friend

reminded me that I was still a deranged psychopath that used to kill prostitutes, hitchhikers, truck drivers, and all other kind of un suspecting people up until now. I couldn't argue with that logic. He was right. I have always been a very fucked up person, and I am still very fucked up either way seeing as how I still kill people . Whether they deserve it or not, it is still morally wrong to kill pe ople. I don't fear the judgment of god since I don't even believe i n him, but I cannot argue with facts. I am a killer. A heinous, mer ciless, disgusting, and depraved killer that talks to his imaginary friend who may or may not really be there. I have an unstoppabl e thirst for blood and it will not stop until I am dead and buried. I thanked him for the reminder and continued on. After I had finish ed checking things out, I went on my way back to the house. As I left the neighborhood, I heard a noise. It was the daughter ope ning the front door. She walked outside with a trash bag. I looke d back on time for us to make eye contact. She almost looked at me as if she knew what I had done. I can't be sure, but it really s eemed like she knew who I was and what I had done. She smile d and waved at me.... I waved back, smiled, turned around, and walked away. Does she know? "You had better find out! The bitc h will give us away!" screamed my friend. He was right.

11.

I have a voice mail on my answering machine telling me that I h ave an appointment with my shrink at 9:00 AM on Friday. Well, t hat's a bit of good news I suppose. I love my visits with my shrin k. She is always good for a laugh. If it weren't for the fact that sh e is disgustingly hot I wouldn't even attempt to go see her. The l ast shrink I had was a shrew of an old woman. She was about fi ve foot one inches tall, and about 300 something pounds. I am n ot one to make fun of someone because of their weight or height but she resembled that of a troll or ogre. She had a cluster of m oles on her face, jagged, browning teeth, and chin hair. She nev er tried, to help me get better. She would make statements like " You never take responsibility for your own actions! You act as if your mental condition is an excuse to act the way you do! No wo nder your grandparents left you!" Yeah, she was a lot of help! W ell, that relationship ended when she went on vacation and neve r came back. I will neither confirm nor deny your suspicions. Wel l, back to my current shrink. The great thing about seeing these people is that they are so naïve. All you have to do is spout out t he right bullshit and squeeze out a tear for them to think you're making progress. She is about an inch or two shorter than I am, has mesmerizing green eyes, ruby lips, and strawberry blonde h air. She is always in a great mood and has lots of energy about her. I tell her things like I am not sexually attracted to anything. And other harmless lies so she never truly suspects that I would possibly have a fascination with her. She always wears these dr esses that have the slit up the side so when she sits down, I can almost see up to her panties. Just enough to leave some to the i magination. She wears the knee high stockings with the line up t he back in the middle and always wears high heels. I think sh e does this on purpose to entice her clients to be honest with he r. As if that is somehow going to help them land in bed with her or something! Ha! If she only knew what I really felt like or thoug ht, she wouldn't be my doctor. I am sure she would feel extremel y uncomfortable knowing that I have fantasized about getting a pair of her panties and wearing them around the house listening to Depeche Modes' "Personal Jesus" masturbating and ejaculati ng into the panties before putting them straight into the washing machine only to do it again the next day. I think if I am ever caug ht, I will ask her to come visit me in prison, tell her how I feel, an d possibly steal a kiss before the guards kick the shit out of me and she never returns. I'm pretty sure that whoever ends up rea ding this at this point is probably reeling from the idea that some one would listen to that song but, FUCK YOU! I like them! I love that song! And I am the one writing in this journal, you chose to r ead it, so shut the hell up! Anyways, I really look forward to our li ttle one hour, twice a month visits.

12.

11:30 AM- I had a wonderful chat with my shrink today. She stat ed that I seemed to be content for once and that I may be comin

g to a point where I may no longer need to come see her as ofte
n. I thought to myself, she must really have no idea how to do h
er job seeing as how she is saying this to a serial killer, but I digr
ess. This comes as a bit of a shock to me and instantly brings s
adness to my heart. If she stops seeing me, then, if I need to se
e a shrink again, chances are they will assign me a new one. Th
at doesn’t work for me. Perhaps I should go to the mall, take off
all of my clothes and shit in the fountain. It may work, but I am al
so afraid they will just lock me up. So, I guess I could start talkin
g about having nightmares and feelings of overwhelming guilt ov
er what my family has gone through. I will have to think of somet
hing soon though. Guess I have two weeks to figure it out. For n
ow, I need to get some sleep before I start my shift.

7:00 PM- I was awakened a bit early by my friend looming over
me with the craziest look I have ever seen him have. “Hey budd
y! When are we going to kill someone again!?!? That was so fun
!” I told him, I wasn’t really sure, I don’t just plan on these kinds
of things, they just sort of land in my lap. “Well, you need to up t
he ante then, my oh so fun to be around chum! Tomorrow is Sat
urday after all, and this we have all weekend, let’s find some fun
to get into!”

13.

3:00 PM- Well, I had a long night followed by a longer than I act ually would have ever wanted day. I am very tired of my “friend”. All he did all last night and most of today is point out and insist I kill people. He pointed out an overweight lady and said she wore makeup too thick, wore too small of clothing, and looked like a sl eazy person, therefore I must kill her. “She obviously doesn’t car e about herself enough to stop showing everyone how little she r espects herself, so we would be doing her and the rest of huma nity a favor” He says while scratching his neck and chewing on his fingernails much like a junkie trying to maintain when they ca n’t just shoot up. “Man, you need to calm down”. I said to him. “Y ou are acting up enough to where I’m halfway sure someone is actually going to see you too!" He just laughed at me and said in his menacing metallic voice. "Oh, I'll calm down alright, just wait till you least expect it, I am going to figure out some way, someday, how to gain full control of you and then the fun will never have to stop!" This kind of troubles me to be honest. Is it possible that I can be controlled by my friend? I realize I'm not the picture of mental health, I'm sure as hell not a hero that is wrestling with my demons and trying to be a better person. But I sure as shit don't want to be possessed by some crazed, bloodthirsty demon or whatever the hell he really is. I often wonder if he is actually there, or a figment of my imagination. Unfortunately, neither would really make a difference. I still see and hear him crystal clear. To me, he is there. No question about it. Some time at about lunch time, I was getting on the bus and of course, as if someone just placed this person in my path, my next victim bumped into me. She was obviously in a hurry to get on the bus before anyone else judging by the way she politely shoved me by the face and told me to "get the fuck out of the way". It wasn't what she did to me that bothered me. It was her whole being. Now, I'm not a racist person. I don't care what color someone is, what they look like, or how much money they make. No, this person, reeked of crack smoke, she looked like she hadn't bathed in days, she had the same twitch my friend had all day, and maybe she just reminded me of him. I don't know for sure what really motivated me between the aforementioned offenses, the way she referred to EVERYONE around her in only racial slurs. Fucking disgusting if you ask me. It wasn't even really enough to make it an OK thing to do t o kill this person. But sure as shit, I followed her off the bus, into the alleyway she crept into, and watched her purchase maybe t wenty dollars in crack from the local dealer. I took a clue, the sm all amount she got for twenty, wouldn't last her more than an ho ur. So, I went up to the dealer, using the same slang she was us ing, I was able to score about fifty bucks worth and was off in th e direction she went making it as inconspicuous as I could so as not to let her know I was following her the whole time. She was ducked over by a dumpster trying to get as much out of that rock in her makeshift pipe as humanly possible. I leaned over and as ked her if she wanted some of mine. I told her I broke my pipe e arlier and I wanted to hit it before the withdrawals kicked in. She of course agreed to share her pipe if I gave her half of what I ha d and we ducked into an abandoned apartment complex across the way. Once inside, she turned to me and said that I was a rea lly nice looking guy and she wanted to have a little fun with me b efore we smoked. I was instantly grossed out by her proposition. She started doing a half-assed strip tease, ended up on her kne es in front of me, and started undoing my buckle. I stopped her and said I wanted to get high before we played around beca use I was jonesing too bad to concentrate. She smiled, her teeth were black with rot. She then pulled the pipe out of her pocket a nd asked me for the crack. I gave her the bag which was just on e of those tiny zip-lock bags. I watched as she took it out, crush ed it up on the ground with her foot, and then loaded the pipe. S he took a big hit off of it, and handed it to me. I grabbed her by t he hair and pulled back really hard. She seemed to be turned on by the force I was using and opened her mouth as one does when they are really excited. I then crammed the still smoking pipe into her mouth and forced it shut. I heard the glass crunch between her teeth. She tried to let out a scream but before she could, I threw her to the ground and started kicking her in the face and the jaw. Blood instantly started pouring out of her mouth and her screams were soon muffled by the amount of blood in her mouth and throat. I could see shards of glass jamming their way out through her throat and then finally, after what seemed like hours, she laid motionless on the ground. I stuffed her body into a hole in the wall a few feet away and covered up the blood with some old newspapers. I was lucky enough that this seemed to be one of those places used as a shelter for many homeless people and there was a bucket of piss and shit over in the corner. I dumped the contents of the bucket onto the newspapers seeing as how there is a high concentration of ammonia in it and that will at least render any of the evidence as inadmissible in court. I made sure I left no trace of my being at the scene and snuck out through another door. I think I will go ahead and relax for the rest of the evening. Of course, my friend got his way and will probably leave me alone for a couple days now.

Chapter 3 – Unthinkable

14.

6:15AM – I was awakened quite violently this morning at about 3 . There was a commotion happening upstairs. I heard screaming , things breaking, and then a loud thud that shook the house. I h eard one of the kids scream, but it was silenced as fast as it had happened. Now, normally I would stay away from something lik e this out of pure principle. I normally would just keep to myself so as not to get any attention. I like to keep a sort of anonymity and that is easier to maintain when barely anyone knows who y ou are, let alone your comings and goings. But not this time, this felt different. I felt compelled to investigate the shitstorm that ha d just went on upstairs. The fact that it was all silent so quickly, made me curious. I know what they say about the cat, but, I just couldn't let it be. I snuck up the stairs to her front door, I hear nothing, nobody moving around, not even a child running about. It made me extremely uneasy. Upon entering the house, I co uld see that the kitchen was strewn with streaks of blood. One of the kids was laying lifeless. I could see that the child was kille d by what looked like a bite on the neck. I heard a noise come from the bathroom down the hall. I carefully investigated the noise. While going do the hall, I looked into the kids' room and saw that the other child was literally in pieces. I was almost disturbed by what I saw, but I think the shock of what I was seeing was too much to comprehend for me at the moment. It's not like I haven't seen a dead body before, seeing as how I am what I am, but the fact that this was once, hell this morning, a walking talking, nuisance, capable of only thinking of what cereal they wanted to eat, and that they wanted to watch SpongeBob…. I was just not expecting to see her in such a state. At this point, I had come to the conclusion that the hooker probably brought in a "customer" that went nuts and she killed him, or he killed her and her kids. Not a far stretch if you ask me. I digress. I went to where the noise was coming from, it sounded like slurping, and sloppy chewing. I could hear heavy breathing. This set me complete into unease. I slowly, and as quietly as I could, opened the bathroom door. What I saw was something I had never in my life expected to see. The hooker was laying on the ground, her head barely attached due to the person in there with her eating most of her neck. He looked up at me with this blank look on his face, his eyes were completely black and lifeless, but he was obviously aware I was there. He got to his feet faster than I could react. He came at me like a crazed animal! I barely got away from him enough to keep him from biting my arm I put up to defend myself. We struggled in the hall and ended up in the living room. Looked quickly around the house, in the kitchen, on the counter,

there was a heavy duty looking ash tray, as I made my way to t
he kitchen, I stumbled and tripped over the child's body. Slipping
in his blood, I noticed the kid started to move. The next thing I k
new, I had to of these crazy Fucks starting to corner me in the ki
tchen. I grabbed the ash tray and smashed the kid in the face. It
didn't even slow him down. So I smashed him repeatedly until hi
s skull gave way, and his body fell backwards, lifeless. The ot
her guy was slipping in blood and brain matter, I grabbed a ham
mer out of one of the drawers and killed him with a single blow t
o the head. Shaking, I took one of the cigarettes next to where t
he ash tray was, and lit it up. As I took a long drag off of the ciga
rette, I heard a gurgling growl come from back in the hall
way. I took the hammer and went to investigate. The woman fro
m the bathroom was trying to crawl her way into the living room.
I put her out of her misery and went into the kids' room wher
e I finished the little girl off as well. I have no idea what is happe
ning, but I am going to see what's happening on the news, ar
m myself in case. I will make another entry when I am sure of
what's really happening.

4:00PM – I am in complete shock of what I saw on the news. Ap
parently, there is an outbreak of some fucked up virus causi
ng people to turn into blood thirsty, angry, cannibalistic animals.
They described the disease as a mutated form of rabies. Nobod
y has any idea how it started, but there are already thousands of
casualties. The hospitals have started to turn away all people wit

h bites or scratches from attacks. This is because apparently, th e person who is bitten and doesn't die right away, turns withi n hours, and there is no cure for this disease. The people who d o die from the attack, come back between minutes, and hours, b ut one thing is certain. They do come back, and they are not the mselves. Other news shows are going off the air until the proble m subsides, getting themselves and their loved ones t o safety. All of the religious channels are alive with televangelist s casting judgment upon all who are listening. I saw one that was live, where the preacher killed himself with a gunshot to the head. All over T.V. and outside, was chaos. There were people outside in the neighbor-hood, looting houses for supplies, then p acking them into their vehicles and driving away. I am really uns ure as to what I should do. I think I will attempt to leave this plac e once there are less people around. Until then, I am going to prepare my bugout bag and try to rest up. I don't know when the next time I am going to be able to sit down will be, so I will wait u ntil I absolutely have to go. For all I know, this could be my last entry. So, it's been fun.....

Chapter 4 – Safety?

15.

I was awakened by a couple of people knocking loudly on my door trying to get in and away from what was happening outside. There was utter chaos outside, and I don't know why, but I let them in. I guess I was just feeling charitable or some shit. But it's whatever. They said that they had been trying to find somewhere safe all night and they saw a light on in my house and everything seemed quiet enough. I told them both to be quiet and get some sleep. So far they don't seem to have brought any attention to the place, so I assume that all is well, at least for the night. They said that they had a vehicle a few miles from here and plan on trying to get to it in the morning. They offered me a ride if we get to it. I suppose I will go ahead and take them up on their offer. I don't really want to get stuck here trying to escape alone. Better to have bait if anything. I bet if they saw what I was writing, this would probably not go too well. Good night for now.

16.

We left a little before 5AM. Trying to take advantage of the low amount of crazies running around. I am still at a loss for words as to what is actually going on. It does seem an awful lot like there is some sort of rabies like behavior in the people affected. I d on't really like the term “Zombie”. It seems to indicate that I am wrong about the existence of God or the Devil. Not to mention, they don't seem to be the stereotypical zombies you would see in the movies. Some of them use weapons, albeit very crudely. I saw one swinging a machete wildly and it took the arm off of one that was standing too close. It seems like they don't register pain seeing as how the one who got her arm cut off, just kept on trying to eat the person they had cornered as if nothing happened. They don't seem to bleed like someone alive either. But they do have a sort of intelligence enough to know the difference between themselves and the “living”. They don't even look at each other, but if there is someone normal running around, they home in on them, like they can smell them or something. They are attracted to sound, light, and movement it seems. Though how they discern between living and well, whatever the fuck they are, is beyond my comprehension. We made it about two miles before we ran out of luck. The couple I was running with had gotten into a bit of a disagreement as to which way to go next due to the high concentration of the zombies in the area we needed to cross. Her husband, seemed to think that the best solution would be to act like this is a zombie movie and pretend to be like them. He figured that they would just let us walk through if they thought we were what they are. Well, I obviously had to disagree with him as did his wife. I told him I had noticed that they literally don't even look at each other which lead me to believe that they may have a certain smell, or something else that we do not understand, that only they can recognize. Fortun

ately, he listened to me. We climbed a ladder up to the roof of w
hat seemed to be a warehouse. There were a couple deadies o
n the roof, I quickly dispatched one of them with a baseball bat t
hat one of them must have had with them when they escaped
up the ladder. These things do not seem to climb or pay much at
tention to the rooftops. I'm not saying they won't notice if I start s
creaming at them and get their attention, but they don't active
ly look around or anything. There must be a radius limit of some
sort with them. Like I said, these are just observations I hav
e made and chosen to write down, for maybe some sort of tactic
al advantage. I will write more as I learn. Looking down from th
e rooftop, we noticed there was a small group that seemed to b
e attempting the whole "look and smell like them" trick that the h
usband had suggested earlier. His wife was resting up a bit sinc
e she was a bit heavy set and obviously not accustomed to
running for long distances. Maybe this is why people should stay
in shape? Haha! Oh well. Anyways, they had adorned themselv
es with what looked like guts or blood or something. I assum
e it was from a zombie they killed. They tried their best to walk a
nd move like the rest of the horde. One of the people noticed
us watching them. As he looked up at us, he nudged his friend
closest to him, who in turn looked up as well. Unfortunately, their
odd movements got the attention of some of the zombies and, w
ell, let's just say they didn't make it. And of course that also brou
ght attention to the fact we were up on the roof. I was correc
t that they wouldn't climb up after us, but they definitely don't
lose interest easily either. I am going to have to figure out a way

to get past these fuckers and to the vehicle they have waiting at the gas station a mile from here. For now, we are going to fo rtify the area, get some rest, and come up with a plan to escape. I don't care if I have to sacrifice one of them to make it. Hell, I don't care if neither of them make it, but I am unsure as to whi ch of them have the keys, or where exactly this car is. I will have to find out.

17.

Everything was chaos this morning. The Zombies did not disper se as we though they would. I woke up with one of the bastard s staring at me trying to climb up to the roof on a pile of more zo mbies. If anything has been learned, it is this; these fuckers wil l not stop once they know you’re there. I kicked the zombie in the face and he fell back down to the ground and splattered the back of his head. The other zombies saw it and it seemed to infuriate them. They started screaming and clawing towards me. This woke the couple that was sleeping peacefully. They of course panicked and instantly, the husband blamed me. I of course told him to shut the fuck up, which instantly reminded me of how much of a pussy I look like. I am about half this guys’ size. But whatever. We were too busy to get into any more than a verbal confrontation. I took one of the radios we had and turned it on high volume. Threw it into the side of a nearby hill. There was grass there and I hoped it wouldn’t break when it hit. It didn’t thankfully. I got on the other end and started to talk loudly into it hoping that it would start to get the mobs’ attention and maybe it would distract them long enough to catch us a break. After about 10 minutes, it seemed to at least take their attention away from the roof. I kept talking on it until we were able to go to the other side of the roof and climb down. There were still quite a few stragglers out in the open between us and what we hoped was freedom. We dodged our way through the mob being sure not to get close enough for one of them to grab us. As we finally approached the awaiting vehicle, the couple got really quiet. I think they were plotting on leaving me there to die and allow them an easy escape. That’s when my friend appeared to me. He looked like he was just as nervous as I was. I wondered why he would feel nervous seeing as how he can’t die. He went on to tell me what I already suspected. They planned on getting me to help them put their stuff in the trunk and as soon as I closed it, they would take off. But what they didn't bet on was that I was one step ahead of them and already took their handgun they failed to tell me they had, and also, the keys. HA! I thought. This is not their fucking day. I shot the husband in the back of the head. As his lifeless body fell to the ground, I could hear the wife screaming, as if I care. She figured she'd get all heroic, which didn't end well for her. I shot her in the knee and kicked her in the chest. When she fell, she was face to face with her newly departed husband. As if she accepted her fate, she cried holding onto her husband. I got in the car, and it took long enough to get the car started where I got a front row seat to watch her starting to get devoured by what was now about ten zombies. I didn't really take the time to count, so don't quote me on just how many there were. As I drove off, all I could think about was the fact that she died almost exactly as I had dispatched my first friend.

18.

I drove for hours until the gas ran out, and found a gas station. It was out in the middle of nowhere, but I was not about to take a stupid risk and use a gun. I have watched enough movies, and based off of how these things seem to react, I chose the crowba r in the trunk, and put the gun in my waistband in case I got corn ered. I went to put gas in the tank when I realized this was one o f those places where you had to go in and have the attenda nt turn the pump on. Unfortunately, it was also the kind of place where if someone pulled the lever up on the pump, it made the b eeping noise to let the attendant know there was someon e trying to fuel up. Probably from before "gas and goes" got popular with the lower income folks. The gas stations started ma king people come in a pay first, before they could have it tur ned on. SO, of course the beeping noise woke up every fucking thing in the building. I had literally not enough gas to get to the next station 50 miles away, so I had two choices to make. One choice was to just start running down the road and hope I r un across another means of shelter, or vehicle, or.... Go into the gas station, assess the situation (how many, can I escape q uick enough, will I have time to fuel up before I have to book it, e tc.), then get what needed to be done over with. Well, I chose do or number two. Obviously, I am still alive since I am writing in thi s journal, so.... SPOILER ALERT! Haha! Anyways... I went into the building using the front door. The place was in disarray. The soda fountain was a mess, there was soda and blood mixed into sticky pools on the floor. Bloody handprints and footprints pretty much everywhere. I decided to do what any law abiding citizen would do and grabbed as many snacks and drinks as I could an d stuffed them haphazardly into my backpack. I also grabbed pain relievers, bandages, ointment, and other stuff I figured w ould come in handy. As I said before, the assholes in the building were awake, so it wasn't as if this was a leisurely encounter. I had to kill two of them right away as I entered the building. One of them was wearing a polo shirt with the logo from the station on it, the other one was wearing board shorts and flip-flops. As I was reaching over the counter to unlatch the door so I could turn on the gas pump outside, one of the bastards came out the bathroom with his pants to his ankles. Really classy. After dispatching the three zombies I ran into, I grabbed everything I needed, and got outside. As I was pumping gas, a couple of zombies came from around the back of the building, I quickly got rid of them as the vehicle was being filled up and got out of the area quickly. As I was driving away, I could see there were more of them closing in on the place. It's a good thing I got out of there when I did.

19.

So, it's been a couple weeks since I have written in this journal. I figure I might as well go ahead and write this down while I have the free time. After the gas station, I found a little farm out in the middle of nowhere and crashed out there for about a week before I ran into any issues. Surprisingly, the issue was not with the zombies, but it was with people. I say this sarcastically of course.

We all know I am not a big fan of people. I don’t feel too guilty when killing zombies for obvious reasons, but I feel even less sh itty about killing people especially because the whole apocalyps e thing has really brought out the true nature of the human race. People will lie, cheat, kill, and steal to get what they want/need. I would sooner trust a honey badger with a sleeping baby, then t o turn my back on anyone living in this world. Either way, I am straying from the story.

I never liked to hunt or kill animals before the whole zombie thin g happened. But now, since there is no easy way to make sure I get the nutrition I need to sustain my health, I guess we do wha t is necessary for survival. Well, it turns out I am pretty da mn good at it. During my exploration of the property, I found a shed. In that shed was a damn arsenal of weapons, ammo, tra ps, knives, you name it. I of course helped myself to what I c ould easily carry with me into the woods, not to mention quietly. I laid out some bear traps and snares in some places that seem ed to have a lot of deer tracks and was open enough to where I would have no trouble subduing the animal after it has been cau ght in my trap. I took the bow out, and an arrow. I drew one back to see how much resistance I would be trying to hold steady gett ing my aim. It didn’t seem to be too much to handle thankfully. I had about 6 arrows that I could find, so I was hoping I would be able to get the job done without missing. After sitting in a nea rby tree for a couple hours, a fawn stumbled into my snare. It ins tantly panicked and started making a lot of noise. I steeled my

nerves, and drew an arrow back. I hit it right in the heart. I don't
know if it's beginners' luck, or if I am just a natural! Either way, I
was awesome! Just saying. Anyways. I climbed down from th
e tree and finished the deer off with a quick slice of the jugular.
After it seemed to have bled out enough to be transported, I thre
w it up on my shoulders and carried it to the shed. I skinned a
nd butchered the animal so I could cook and eat it. I found a bun
ch of canned goods in the pantry so I had something to go wit
h it, and there was a wood stove, so cooking was pretty easy
to accomplish. After a much deserved meal, I went further into t
he house and stumbled upon a wine cellar. "I could really get
used to this place". I said to myself, out loud. Which seemed to
have triggered my friend to appear. He told me, there is no way I
can ever consider something like this as permanent. Someda
y, probably soon, more people would come, or zombies, or both,
either way, we will never be safe. I looked at my friend and sai
d "what do you mean US? It's not like you can die, it's not like
you will feel the flesh rip from your bones when the zombies fea
st on you, you won't end up like them if there is enough of you
left to get up and walk. SO WHAT THE FUCK GIVESYOU THE
RIGHT TO SAY THE WORD US?! NOTHING! YOU ARE A FIG
MENT OF MY FUCKING IMAGINATION! A FUCKING FAIRYT
ALE! FUCK OFF!!" This of course didn't go too well. He then p
roceeded to explain to me in a very calm, and annoying tone, th
at if he was a figment of my imagination, that I would be
able to will him away... I would be able to concentrate really har
d, and he would just disappear. He taunted me for about an ho

ur before I finally got sick enough of his constant mockery, and I tried. Of course it didn't work. He assured me that from this point on, he will not be leaving me. I will be stuck with him, until the bitter end. He wants me to stay alive due to the fact that if I die, so does he. And he isn't ready to die quite yet. So, I guess I am stuck with him… Joy.

After a couple days of toiling and surviving, not to mention tolerating the growingly annoying babbling of my friend on subjects ranging from the weather, to how he misses the fun of hunting humans and the satisfaction that comes from the kill. I was out hunting again. Looking for another deer, or maybe something smaller. It is getting harder to keep the meat from spoiling. There is electricity at the time, and there is a generator here, so if I can find some gas station nearby, then maybe I can make sure it works and possibly stay here longer, I don't know though due to how things have gone in movies and TV shows, usually, nothing lasts very long. Either way, it doesn't hurt to try to prepare for an extended stay. The fridge seems to be running out of Freon, which is why I am worried about the meat spoiling. Either way, I was hunting. While I was climbing the same tree I caught my last deer I noticed there was a small group of people working their way through the forest. I instantly thought to myself, that if they found my place, they would definitely try to take it from me. So I devised the best plan I could in the little time that I could. I needed to separate the group and then take them out one by one, preferably, without the rest noticing until it's too late. My friend sug gested that I use some of the traps I had originally laid out for ca tching food. I told him that I thought it was a pretty stupid idea since I needed to catch them by surprise. There were four of the m. Three men, and a female. She had her face covered up in a scarf so I couldn't see her face, but I could tell by the way she carried herself and her build in general. She had several layer s of clothes, so it would have been hard to tell if you weren't look ing hard enough. They were all armed, one had a rifle, the other two men had rather stout looking shotguns, while the woman, ha d a sizeable revolver. They were wearing bulletproof vests, t hat were covered in filth, blood, and god knows what else. It was obvious that they had been through a lot to get to this point, wh ich put me at an even higher rate of panic, because that meant t o me, that if they saw me, they would most likely shoot first than to talk to me. The first one I took out, was the younger of the me n. He looked to be in his late teens, early twenties. He ventured off near the small creek about a hundred feet from the group. He went to take a piss, I snuck up behind him as he whistled what s ounded like Für Elise by Beethoven, and drove my knife into his back, through his lung, while holding a hand over his mouth and nose so as to keeps him from screaming out to his friend s. I gently let him down to the ground when he stopped strugglin g. It took very little to take out the bigger guy. He was obviousl y a lot stronger than I was, physically at least. I waited till he was alone. The others went out looking for their missing partner whil e he stayed and set up camp. Fortunately, they hadn't ve ntured much further than when I first noticed them. I took him do wn with a clean shot from my bow to the head. I dragged his bo dy into the tent in case anyone walked back before I was finis hed. The other two were trickier. I had originally planned on taki ng them out one after the other, but my friend suggested that too much could go wrong since they were both armed. I couldn't help but agree with him. I set up bear traps around the campsite and waited. I figured with the distraction, that one of them wo uld get caught, the other would run to their aid, and I would be able to kill them both with two arrows before they would get the chance to react. The plan worked for the most part, with the fact that his screaming was incredibly loud. He of course got the atte ntion of a group of zombies. I snuck away, and hopefully the bi ters will all dissipate by the morning. Until then, I took their weap ons I could grab quickly, and their bags which had food, bandag es, and ammo, also, one of them had some cigarettes, which wa s nice, I hadn't had one in a long time. It felt so good to feel th e smoke go into my lungs. They were a bit stale, but I wasn't go nna bitch about it. I ate, and now, I am going to rest up for mo re hunting, and maybe scavenge what's left of their campsite if it 's safe to do so in the morning.

20.

I woke up the next morning to a tapping sound coming from one of the windows downstairs. Upon further investigation, it turn ed out to be a group of zombies. I wasn't worried at first, they ha dn't noticed me, and so I went back upstairs to get a better look at what I was doing. I went to the balcony in the front of the house. There weren't any signs of the dead out front, so I was able to climb up to the roof without being detected. To my dismay, there were what seemed to be hundreds of the fuckers in the back yard. I packed up what I could into the car, I tossed a couple flares that I found in the bags of the group from the day before. They provided the distraction I needed to get the gear into the car and take off. At this point, I am pretty sure there is no place that I will be able to stay safe on a permanent basis. I am alone. I will always be alone. If it weren't for the fact that I was afraid of death, I would have just killed myself at this point. Instead, here I am. Still writing in this stupid fucking journal, still talking to a figment of my imagination, still killing people who get close enough to me, and still, not sure what to think of this situation. I don't understand. If there is a god, then this is the end of the world. If there is a god, then this is the apocalypse and those of us that are still living, are being punished. But it doesn't make any fucking sense. I understand, that I would be someone who would deserve such a fate, but I have to believe, through logic, that there are others who are actually surviving, who have what's left of their families with them, to include children, elders, whatever. This is to say that God is punishing them too right? What a loving cunt God is. I am an atheist, but if I was a religious person, then I would really be questioning my logic at this point. This is a fucking crock of shit. All I can do is survive. Fuck it. I think I will kill myself tomorrow. Or at least try. I'll probably pussy out though. Whatever.

Chapter 5 – I Had a Dream

21.

I keep having this dream lately. I keep hearing the voice of my m other calling me. I am a child in this dream, running through the house looking for her. Every time I get closer to her voice, it relo cates to another place in the house. This repeats over and ove r until I end up in a dark room. The door slams shut and there in that rooms is the body of my friend whom I killed so long ago. C overed in dirt and old blood, half rotted and half eaten. He turn s to me, opens his eyes, and screams a blood curdling scream . I wake up at this point. I am always covered in sweat after this dream. I don't really understand what this is supposed t o mean. I am not one of those dipshits that keep a dream journa l, whatever the fuck that is. I don't have any way of knowing wha t the hell this means. Perhaps it's my friends' way of messing w ith me. He is always there, staring at me while I sleep. I wake up , he's there staring at me. He can go days where all he does is watch, and not say a damn thing to me. Other times, it's non-stop babbling about stupid shit. I really wish I could get rid of hi m, but, I cannot. I am at a loss.

22.

When I was running out of gas, I was in luck this time. I was on the highway and there was a gas station right off the exit. I was pretty much able to get the gas and snack run done with minimal zombie combat. There were maybe three of them at this one. All of them were trapped in the store. I easily dispatched them as they fought to be the first out the door I opened. They are definitely not smart. Almost comically stupid at this point. I laughed harder than I should have as they fought to get out. It was like they were getting mad because they couldn't get out the door, but they weren't smart enough to figure out why. It reminded me of the stooges show my grandpa used to watch all the time. I often wonder what life would have been like if I was a normal kid. I have always been pretty upset at how easily my grandparents let me go. It's not like sitting here whining about it is going to do me any good now is it?

23.

After a few hours on the road, I got tired and needed to find somewhere to sleep. I thought about pulling over to the side of th

e road and locking the door, but I came to my senses. I mean, it’
s a main highway, so the chances of someone, or somethin
g, finding me whilst I sleep is greater if I stay there, so I found a
side-road and parked where I could get out in a hurry if needed.
I left the car running and the music going. I was listening to
“Crystal Ship” by the Doors as I drifted away to sleep. I always l
oved music. Especially the Doors. Jim Morrison was obviously i
nsane, but such a poetic genius. I loved every song and poe
m on that CD I had. It was a greatest hits CD, so, it had nothing
but good songs. Anyways, I remember the very moment I fell asl
eep. The music was the only thing I could hear in the darkness.
There was a light at the end of the darkness, so I started walkin
g towards it. The closer to the light I would get, the more the mu
sic would fade out, and I could hear someone sobbing, getting
louder and clearer as I got closer. The light was coming from a d
im night light. It was one of those angel shaped, plugin types of
night lights. I looked about it and found a light switch. As I went t
o flip the switch, a voice behind me, familiar, yet strangely differ
ent, spoke. “Be careful gazing into the darkness. It gazes into y
ou as well”. I didn’t decide to hit the switch just yet. I turned arou
nd and tried to discern where the voice came from. It sounded l
ike a woman, but there was another voice along with it, as if ther
e were two people saying something at the same exact time. I tri
ed to speak out, but found I was unable to speak at all. I start
ed to feel as though I was being held tight, in that one spot, u
nable to move, unable to turn my head, or close my eyes. I tried
to scream, but nothing came out. Out of the darkness came m

y psychiatrist. What was she doing here I wondered. As she ca
me closer, I realized she wasn't the same. Her eyes were compl
etely black, as were her teeth. She was pale, more pale than sh
e was last time I saw her. She spoke. "Just let go. There is nothi
ng left for you here. Just pain, and death. Just madness. You
have no reason to live in this world. You have nothing to give to
the world. You're just a killer, a cancer, an illness in an already s
ick world." Her voice became more and more demonic sound
ing as she continued to speak. "What's wrong baby? Why did y
ou kill your friend? Why do you continue to kill people? Just kill y
ourself. Kill yourself! KILL YOURSELF!!! DO IT!!!!!" I awoke. C
overed in sweat, and yet, cold. I looked around to see that there
were zombies all around the vehicle. They must not have notice
d I was in there, or alive. I wasn't about to try to figure it out a
t that moment. So I quickly put the car into drive, and drove thro
ugh the small group. I made it about three miles or so before I
heard and felt something I really didn't want to. There was a lou
d boom noise, and of course, the flopping sound the tire makes
when it goes flat. What a great day this is turning out to be. I will
grab what I can and try to find my way to safety, or somethin
g. Wish me luck.

Chapter 5 – The Dream is a Nightmare

Well, I was walking and minding my own business, when a group of people in one of those high end conversion vans, the one with the TV, fridge, and other bells and whistles, whatever. Any ways, they offered to let me join them as far as they were going. There were 3 people in the van. Two women one was red headed, she seemed to be in her thirties, the other was I assumed in her early teens. The boy that was with them, was actually smaller than I am. He looked like he was barely out of his teens. By the way they razzed him for most of the ride, I assumed he was the younger girls' brother. They were actually kind of tolerable, with the exception of the boy. He was whiney, and demanded we listen to his shitty fucking "music". It was some horrid shit that sounded like a bitchy teenager crying about his girlfriend breaking up with him and him wanting to cut his own heart out. I never understood what happened to metal. It used to be hardcore, like Cannibal Corpse, Slayer, or even Iron Maiden. but not this shit he was listening to. This is one of those things that make me glad this is end of society. I will no longer have to listen to these new "artists" destroy what's left of music. Horseshit.

I digress. I fell asleep for a while. I didn't dream this time. My friend, was sitting next to me when I awoke. He was looking disgustedly at the boy. I didn't want to ask him what his problem was, mainly because I didn't want to let on that I have an imaginary friend. I just wanted to ride along as far as I could go, and then go my separate way without incident. My guess was that they had a larger group they were trying to get to. They said somethin g about a military base a couple hundred miles away, so I figur ed, that would be a good point to get off and continue my journe y on my own. I wasn't in the mindset to live with other people, wi th my set of issues, I am not a group type person. I didn't have t o say anything to my friend. He looked at me and said "I don't lik e that fucking kid. I say we kill these fucks and take this van fo r ourselves." Before I could even try to respond, he interrupted me. "You don't always have to respond. I can hear your thoug hts buddy. It's like we are becoming more and more connected ." "Great!" I thought, he of course responded to that as well. "No worries buddy! I will never fully take over. I like being the separa te entity. If I took over completely, I would probably get us kille d. I'm just going to help you stay alive as long as you can. Now quick fucking around and listen to me. These people, they are g oing to figure you out, if they don't during this ride, then what? W e walk? To where? To what end? They don't even seem to beli eve their own deluded shit! What do they do when they get t o where they're going, and it's overrun by fucking zombies!? Th en what? We have seen enough movies and TV shows to know what happens next. The group argues, someone gets out of ha nd, and people die. Do you see these people surviving this shit? Hell, I'm not even sure we have what it takes to survive ourselve s! These people are weak, and stupid! They picked your ass up off the side of the highway, and little do they know, that you are a straight out killer! I mean really! You are exactly what they don 't want to pick up. And yet, here you are. HAHA!!! I say do them a favor and save them the grief of being torn asunder by zombie

s. Kill them quick, and be done with it. There isn't anything less polite than saving them the pain." I told him in my mind, to knock it off for a minute and let me think. He quieted down. And I conte mplated what I should do. He was stoic and patient. I guess, sin ce he can read my mind, he knew I agreed with his logic. I just n eeded a plan.

I looked around the vehicle and played things through in my hea d. I thought about just killing the women while the boy kept driving, but I knew they would make enough noise to get his atte ntion, then I would probably end up on the receiving end of the r evolver he had up in the dashboard. I knew I couldn't just kill him while he drove, for obvious safety reasons. Then I thought, maybe I could shoot the women, then make him pull over at gu npoint, and then execute him. But I would need to get my gun out of my bag, and reposition myself closer to him, without maki ng anyone in the vehicle suspicious before I did what I pl anned. So I figured that would go wrong somehow. To my pleas ant surprise, he announced that he needed to stop for gas, an d needed to take a piss. So we pulled into a gas station.

25.

Well, that was unexpected. For the record, I had full intentions of getting rid of everyone I met on this ride, but one lives. I can't sa y I'm all too disappointed either. We got into the gas station with not very much effort, it is a lot easier to clear a building when yo u have three other people assisting. The boy was way more agg ressive than I had expected from looking at him. His capacity for violence rivaled that of mine. Not that he lived, but he really su rprised me. As I was saying, we cleared the building. There w ere about eight or nine zombies in the building, we basically divi ded and conquered. Pretty easy really. I watch him behead a r ather large one in the middle isle of the store near the bread and chips. Needless to say, we didn't get any bread, or chips on our way out. After the front of the store was clear, we spread out lo oking for anything that could be useful. The boy and the older w oman went into the back area where the freezer was to see i f they could find any frozen goods we could salvage since the re is a fridge and microwave in the van. I went into the garage to see if I could find tools. I also planned to lure one of them into t here to kill them off undetected. But, it didn't go the way I planne d, as I said before. I heard a muffled scream come from the free zer area and went to see what the noise was being caused b y. It was the older woman, her clothes were half torn off and the boy was raping her. He had his gun to her head and he kept telli ng her to shut the fuck up.

He didn't hear me sneak in behind him. I swung a wrench at his head. Instantly, there was blood all over the freezer, my face, a nd my clothes. When I hit him, the impact caused him to squeez e the trigger of his gun which was aimed at her face. They were both stone dead. I stood there for a couple seconds. Halfw ay catching my breath, halfway in shock from what had happene

d. I had been the predator, the bad guy, for the entire beginning of whatever this shit is that's going on out here. But at that moment, I had forgotten that there are other monsters out there aside from the zombies, and myself. I heard a noise behind me. I turned around to see the younger girl with a 9mm handgun pointed at me. Her hands were shaking and she had tears in her eyes. She spoke. "I know who you are. I remember you. You were the one who got rid of Jack. The asshole that was raping me on a regular basis. I know what you are, and what you did. You killed people before all this. I knew that was you when you got in the van. I kind of hoped this would happen, aside from what just happened to mom. She always attracted the worst men. I kind of figured it was going to end something like this. I watched you sneak him into the trailer, also, I went there when you left, and saw blood everywhere. I put two and two together. I saw you when you came back the next day too. I waved to you, and you waved back. It's funny how things turned out, isn't it?" She lowered her weapon, and we cleared the store. We got into the van and left. She wasn't really fond of trying to drive, so I drove for the rest of the way to the military base. My friend wasn't too fond of this arrangement, but I told him that he will have to suck it up. She introduced herself on the way, her name is Izzy. Mine, I told her, is Johnny.

My name is Johnny.

Chapter 6 – The Base

26.

After several hours, we finally made it to the exit where the milita
ry base was, I was surprised to say the least, at the amount of
vehicles there were parked for as far as I could see. We would h
ave to walk from there. It took us at least twenty minutes just t
o get to the gates. I felt uneasy. The place looked as though
it had been overrun. There were old, brown bloodstains all over
everything. Bloody handprints and streaks of blood all over wind
ows, doors, and all over the security booth. Against my better ju

dgment, we pressed on further into the base. After another 30 minutes of walking seemingly without hope of finding anyone, we heard a voice over the P.A. system. The voice directed us to walk for another 10 minutes in the direction we were going, and to be mindful that we aren't alone out there. Also, the voice made sure to make it a point to tell us to do exactly as they say when we got to the gate, or they would shoot us. I suppose in these times, that's probably a safety precaution. I could certainly not see them wanting to let anyone dangerous into their safe haven. Right? Shut up! But seriously, what would they know about anyone who walks up to their gates? That person survived this far, who is to say they didn't have to kill a few people to do so? Just saying.

Anyways, we got to the gate. After a little scuffle with some of the zombies that were there, meaning there were about ten or fifteen of the ugly bastards, and they were dispatched by the people in the guard towers, using silenced assault rifles. We were searched, and cleared. They looked at my journal, one of them scoffed and called me a faggot. I don't understand why it was necessary to do that, and apparently, I wasn't the only one who thought that when the other guard snatched the journal back from him and handed it back to me, shooting an evil glance at the dickhead that took it from me. I am so glad he didn't start reading it. I guess I never thought how easily someone could just steal and read it. I shall have to find a good place to hide it if I am to remain in anonymity with what I am. I am still not sure people will be comfortable with a serial killer living among them. From the looks of the place and the people in it, I don't think it would end with them just kicking me out, it would more likely end with my head posted on a makeshift spike, for all to see, as a lesson. "This is what happens to murderous, disgusting pigs!" the people would shout. Or maybe I'm being too paranoid, for all I know, they may actually want someone like me around, because I can get the job done, with little to no help. Either way, I'm not trying to find out. So I will hide it.

27.

Well, I was given the "Grand Tour" as they called it. We started in the garage, which seriously resembled what you would see in one of those post-apocalyptic movies, where the vehicles are heavily armored, and mounted with all sorts of zombie killing amenities. I have to admit, I was extremely impressed with the EOD vehicle that was retrofitted with spikes, and what looked like a flamethrower in the turret bay. The tires somehow looked like they were re-enforced with a type of resin. When I asked about it, they said their mechanics came up with it to keep from getting a flat while out on supply runs. I wasn't going to question too much further about the vehicles, the person giving the tour didn't seem to want to hear any more of my inquisitions. We then went to the common area, where there were couches, tables, and chairs stre wn about. There were working radios and TVs as well, though there was nothing on due to the fall of mankind, I guess no daytime talk shows then! That's a joke, I hated those damn things. They always put the most ignorant shits that they could find, and put them in made up situations for the entertainment of people who might have well been put on the show themselves. Fucking horrible. That, and those fucking "Reality" shows, where they had people get drunk, fight, and fuck for the entertainment of the masses. Sometimes, I look back, and I am glad humanity has fallen. We were a disease in our own rights. Sick, hateful, selfish, always looking for that instant gratification. It seemed to me that the only people that got by, were the one's willing to fuck everyone else over to get what they wanted. The rich, wanted to get richer, by making the poor, poorer. Not one fuck given for the person starving in the alleyways. Not one care for the child that went hungry. Our society was on the outs. Fuck them! But yet, in this new world, money doesn't have power anymore. Not that I can see anyways. What is money going to do for you when all there is left is to be eaten and turn into one of those things? You are nothing more than a fucking cheeseburger! What does the fly have to offer the spider in return for its life? Chew on that for a minute….. Anyways, I am straying from the tour, my apologies.

After we left the common area, they took us to the "Mess Hall" as was plainly lettered above the entryway of the dining facility. There were tons of people just eating and talking like this was a normal day like every other day. Laughing, eating, talking with th eir mouths full of food. I looked over where the food was being served, and noticed there were people cooking in the back, and people serving up healthy portions of all sorts of food, there w as pizza, mash potatoes, veggies, even pasta and various sauc es. It was nice to smell familiar food smells, instead of the smell of my own armpits for once. As we left the area, the guys givi ng the tour told us that we had a few more places to go, then we had to meet with the leaders of this new community.

We walked through a long corridor. There were biohazard signs on the doors, and big trash bins with the same symbol on them. Further into the facility, they would show us the quarantined are a, though we could not go in for obvious reasons. The tour-guid e told us, that there are literally hundreds of doctors and scie ntists, working feverishly to find some way to either cure, or at le ast vaccinate and prevent further infection from this disease. I couldn't help but snicker a little bit about it. Only because I truly don't see how they are going to find anything to stop this. It see ms too far-fetched to me. But then again, I don't really know m uch about the subject, so, I suppose I am just being pretentious. It's difficult to hold out hope, when there is literally nothing that g ives me hope. If there was a god, he has abandoned us. He doe sn't love us, and he truly could give a fuck less about what happ ens to us.

Anyways. After we left the medical section, we were shown to th e “War Room”. This, we were told, is where the leaders of the co mmunity plan, and set in motion all that happens, in, and outside of the compound. We were told to sit down, they gave us all b ottles of water, and we were told to wait. We waited for what se emed like an hour. I felt myself doze off, only to wake up to my fr iend looking at me.

“What the fuck are we doing here? I don’t remember saying I wa nted to be part of anything but what WE have together! I don’t re member you even consulting me on joining whatever the shit thi s is!” I said nothing to him, so as not to lead on to anyone that I may or may not be batshit crazy. That would be the last thing I need to do. “But, what if they find out what you are? Then what? It’s not likely that they would want you here knowing that you ar e a killer. It’s definitely not likely that they would let you go free e ither. They will take you out back and shoot you, or worse, use y ou for experiments, before they would do anything else.” He w as right, I thought to myself. Maybe I should leave on my first opportunity. I hate when he makes sense, it makes me feel so o ut of control of my own actions.

I also know that Izzy will be safer here, than with me. Who know s, what if my friend somehow gains control of me, and before I can regain control, he kills her? Why am I even thinking about th is shit? I am so confused as of late. I am not supposed to car e about people. I am a sociopath, or something. What the hell a m I doing giving a shit about a kid I barely know anything about? Whatever. Maybe I’m tired. I’m going to finish this entry, and the n I think I will rest until the right time to leave, hopefully undetected.

Finally, the leaders came into the room. First, there was an older man, he had a rough and tumble look about him. He wore a grey, woolen overcoat over a tattered vest. He had one of those giant mustaches that reminded me of old western movies and he chewed on a huge cigar. His long gray hair hid his eyes, which made me uneasy since I couldn't tell who he was fixated on at the time. He took a seat on the left of three seats at the head of the conference room. Another man walked out, wearing a leather jacket with no shirt underneath, he had long dark hair and a full beard. From what I could see in the dimly lit room, he was covered in tattoos and scars. Some of the scars looked like bite wounds. I can only speculate that there is no way they are from zombie bites. I have not seen anyone NOT turn into one of those things after being bitten. There can't be people immune to this shit right? So far, nobody had said anything. Then the third leader entered the room. All whispers, and anything else that was going on, seemed to stop. At first I thought I was seeing things, but it turns out, I was incorrect. She sat down between her two minions, and scanned the room. She looked more hardened than she did the last time I saw her. She was wearing an eye patch, but her red hair fell over it, covering it for the most part. She had a scar going from above her good eye, to her chin. It looked like a claw mark. She was wearing a black dress with red flowers all over it. It was about knee high. She was wearin

g those stockings I like so much, with a pair of combat boots. Sh
e was also wearing a pair of gloves, and a red scarf. On her
side was a Machete in its sheath, and a revolver in its holster.
She was the only one I could outwardly tell was armed. I assum
ed the other two were as well, but I couldn't see the weapons. S
he motioned for one of the guards at the door to bring her s
omething. He walked over to her right away, and handed her a b
lack clove cigarette. He then lit it for her, and she looked up at hi
m, he backed away, never turning his back on her, or her guard
dogs. She took a long drag, and exhaled, looking at all of us. T
hen, her eyes met mine. I had expected that maybe, she wo
uld have been happy to see someone she knew, but that wasn't
what the look on her face implied, she instantly got extremely ira
te, and screamed at the guards to take me to the "interview
room". Before I knew what was happening, a white flash, and I
was dreaming.

I dreamt. I was in my grandparent's house again, only this time,
there was nobody there. I walked around calling out to my gra
ndpa, or grandma, but no-one answered. Then I heard a door sl
am shut near the entryway. Upon investigation, I saw that a ma
n that looked like a wolf had entered the house. He had th
e face and fur of a wolf, but was standing like a man would. I wa
s actually frightened by this sight, more than I think I have ever b
een afraid of anything in my entire life. I ran, but my legs were h
eavy. I tried to scream out, but couldn't. No voice would come o
ut as I strained to scream. The room went black, and suddenly, t

here my friend stood in front of me. Bloody, and dismembered. He smiled a bloody smile. “Soon, you will have no control!” I was awakened by cold water being dumped on my head. Disoriented, I tried to look around the room. I was handcuffed to a steel folding chair in the middle of an otherwise open room. It was dark with the exception of the light over my head. Her minion with the leather jacket appeared out of the shadows. He introduced himself as Mick. He was polite at first, asking me who I was, and what I was doing there, how I survived, and stuff like that. But then things started getting heated. Apparently, she, knowing who I was, did not feel all too comfortable with one of her former patients, that she was completely convinced was a serial killer as it is, would suddenly show up, where she is, in this kind of a situation, where finding each other again, should be completely impossible. After he struck me enough times to make sure I wasn’t lying about this being dumb luck, and I wasn’t just here because I’m a stalker out to kidnap, and rape, and kill her even though it was more than obvious that even if that was my intention , I wouldn’t succeed. I really couldn’t blame her really. But at the same time, I felt a little bit insulted, and hurt. I mean, I really felt like I had a connection with her. But of course, I’m crazy, so what the fuck would I know right? For the record, since names are being put out and whatnot. I guess it doesn’t really matter what I put in this journal since most of what I was trying to hide is now irrelevant to anything lawful. Society, laws, morals, and money are gone. The only thing there is out here, is survival, and death. So, anyways, her name is Dr. Rebecca Stevens.

Her guard dogs, Mick, and Josiah, interrogated me for what see
med like forever, taking turns, acting one minute, like they didn'
t enjoy what they were doing, and they wanted me out of that sit
uation as soon as possible, to outright calling me names and kic
king the shit out of me. The taste from the dirty barrel of Josiah's
gun is even to this moment, still in my mouth, mixed with blood a
nd toothpaste. It didn't help me that they also cleaned out my s
upplies from my pack, and of course, the journal I'm writing in
now. Dr. Stevens was unimpressed with what she read in the be
ginning, especially with the things I wrote about her. She came i
n and had the guys hold me while she got her disgusted kicks in
. All in all, this could have gone better. But when all was said an
d done. She had read the thing in its entirety. She told me, the
only reason they don't kill me, is because they all see the potenti
al to be an asset to the community in me. She said, the fact that
the only people that were killed were either an absolute threat,
or doing something they shouldn't have, showed that I have at le
ast the ability to discern right from wrong, and mostly, I'll pic
k right. Also, Izzy had begged them to spare me, do to what I
did for her before things went to shit. So I guess, they are going
to continue to watch me very closely, and I guess that means, I
won't be getting out of here for a while at least. Shit.

28.

I woke up this morning. The wounds on my face are starting to h
eal, so of course they're throbbing and itching a whole lot. The
gash above my eyebrow keeps opening back up in my sleep an
d I end up having to carefully peel my face off of my pillow. It f
eels really good to sleep in a bed. It may not be anything more t
han a military bunk, and I have several roommates, but all in all,
I am pretty happy. They put Izzy up with the other females, wh
ich at first she objected to, stating she wanted to stay near me, b
ut of course, they won on that debate thankfully. I am not saying
I don't like being around her, the truth is I like her a lot. Like a li
ttle sister that fully understands me. It's strangely comforting that
I don't have to hide what I am around her, and most of these p
eople, well at least not the good doctor and her watchdogs. The
y decided not to tell everyone else due to the fact that some of t
hem may panic and try to kill me themselves, or, they will not
want to be around me enough where people are going to prot
est my being there. She seems to think I am going to be useful,
she just hasn't told me exactly what use, I am going to be. Toda
y, I am going to hang out and get comfortable, and rest up. To

morrow, I will be going with Mick and Josiah, to learn what the plan is, and what use I have to offer the community. My friend has been oddly quiet, though not gone. He follows me around, almost as if he is pouting. I don’t really understand why he is so docile in this environment. Normally he would be spouting out rhetoric about how we need to get out of this place, and who I need to kill off, and why I am stupid for staying. But no, he says nothing. He barely makes eye contact with me. I am not sure if this is because my sub conscience is calm at the moment, or what to think. I have tried a couple times to talk to him, but he mainly just stares at the floor. He looks almost, sad.

Chapter 7 – Purpose

29.

I was able to sleep pretty well last night aside from the throbbing in my mouth where they knocked one of my molars loose. It w asn't knocked so loose that I may lose it thankfully, but, nonethel ess, it's pretty painful. Anyways, they took me to see Dr. Steven s and crew today where they told me that it was time to start c ontributing to the group. She had a group of people that went ou t and scoured the wasteland for survivors, gear, food, and other supplies. They were all broken into smaller groups. I was to be sent out on the search and rescue team, which also entailed sca venging through the ruins of old neighborhoods for canned good s and other non-expired supplies, and also rescuing survivors if we ran into any. We were to stay in a tight formation and not to s eparate until the group leader stated to do so. They also have Iz zy doing stuff around the base. From what she told me, they wer e having her help out in the lab with cleanup to start with.

I was wrought with nerves on our way off the base. It dawned on me that I haven't stated where I actually was. Well, I guess if yo u're reading this, you can probably do the math ha-ha! But I start ed out in a small town in Michigan on the border of Canada. I wo uld have gone over the border, but they locked that shit down tig ht the night of the outbreak. Some of you know exactly where I a m talking about, and I will neither confirm nor deny the truth L OL! I digress. My friend started to liven up as we left the install ation. “Ooooh! Where we going?!? Can I drive?!?” I just shot a dirty look at him, he smiled at me playfully. I mean seriously! He doesn’t say shit to me for like a week, and now, he wants to start with the jokes?! Anyways, we drove for about an hour out to a remote, but moderately populated (At least when there were people living there) area. There were several cookie-cutter homes with unkempt lawns, and looked like something out of one of those time traveler stories. The neighborhood was being reclaimed by nature. The trees were growing wildly along with what used to be trimmed bushes and gardens. The cars in some of the driveways were grim reminders of the fact that something horrifying had happened there. There were dried up bloodstains and handprints all over windows and doors of the houses and vehicles. Some of the cars had broken windows, and the fact that a struggle had happened right there was obvious. There were half eaten corpses scattered randomly around the neighborhood. I could only think of the events that led up to their demise. I don’t normally get depressed over things I see, but I did make the mistake of looking in one of the vehicles and saw the decomposed remains of a child in their car seat. The window had been broken, and the child eaten in their seat. All that was left was unable to be torn from the seat. I actually got really upset and shed a tear. One of the guys saw it and made a joke about it to one of his friends.

My first instinct was to get him alone and kill him. But I fought that urge off. I am trying to give this a shot. I haven’t ever been co nsidered part of anything. Nobody ever wanted shit to do with me, so this was nice. I laughed it off, and told him to go fuck himself. He laughed and we went back to work. It's funny how that seemingly harmless encounter really almost escalated to someone dying. Maybe there is hope for me after all.

We went through the whole neighborhood in the course of about eight or nine hours. We filled the back of the armored five-ton to the brim with all sorts of goods. Unfortunately, there were no survivors to be found. The guy who made fun of me earlier introduced himself as Jerome. He said that he tries to make a joke out of a lot of things to help him cope with the depression and anger that come from what we as a species are dealing with. "Without humor, without the ability to maintain some sort of humanity, what are we? No better than the zombies." I nodded in agreement. Though, I'm pretty sure he wouldn't be so comfortable talking to me if he knew what I was. All in all, I would say this day has been pretty good. I'm going to go visit Izzy before I head off to bed.

30.

I went to talk to Izzy, but the conversation was cut short. Dr. Stevens called for her to come help in the lab. I waited around and ate. After about an hour, I gave up and walked around. I ran into Mick. I am going to put this out there. I do not trust Mick, Josiah, or Dr. Stevens. They are all too fucking shady for my liking. He looked at me for what seemed like 5 minutes, and spoke. “I don’t know who you are, but I know *what* you are. And to tell you the truth, I don’t fucking like you. Don’t let me catch you slipping little boy, you’ll have an accident and we won’t be able to save you. It is that fucking easy! Know this, Rebecca isn’t going to think twice if I tell her that story. I don’t know why she would even consider having a fucking sick little shit like you around u nless she had some sort of soft spot for you. I am not playing th at game with you. Fuck up, and I will kill you myself." He walked passed me, making sure to put a shoulder into me and bounce me into the wall next to me. "This guy, is going to have to go bu ddy! He said it himself, he plans to kill you, therefore, we need t o take him out as soon as we can." I actually agreed with him. T he issue I have is I still want to know what's up with the bite mar ks on him. Are they from zombies? Or is it something else? If he is somehow immune, and it's important for him to stay alive, t hen I don't think it's the best idea to kill the one person able to c ure the infected. I suppose I'm going to have to do some resea rch before making the decision to do so. I will talk to Izzy and se e if she can help me gain access to the lab at some point, or at l east we can see if there are records on him, and she can see if there is any reason not to take him out. I am also unsure as t o whether I should let her know what my possible plans are. She seems happy here, and I know she knows what I am, but I don't know if she would be all too comfortable with me placing both ou r lives in danger by doing this. I need to think.

31.

Before I could come up with even a thought as to what to say to Izzy, I overheard one of the doctors screaming for help. I of cou rse, being the good citizen I am, ran to help with what I could. A pparently, they were having an issue with one of the zombies in the quarantine section. I was OK with going in and killing it, but that's not what they wanted me to do, they wanted me to catch it alive, and inject it with a sedative. Apparently they are working on a cure, and it's not ready yet. The last shift had forgotten to dose the sleeping zombie. This peaked my curiosity. I mean, that should mean, that this is definitely not, the whole classic case of the undead coming as judgment from "God" to punish the wicked left alive on earth then. This is a disease. A curable one at that from what I am understanding. Anyways, back to what happened. I walked into the quarantined area to see a girl standing over a bloody body. It looked like she was admiring her work. I yelled to get her attention. I wasn't about to just walk up and turn her around like those dipshits that end up getting bit. I maintained my distance. She did not respond to me being in the room at all. My yelling just had not effect on her. So I threw a sample cup that was on the ground at her. She instantly turned around, screamed a blood curdling Warcry, and charged me. The tables and other debris in the way were literally no help for me. She leapt over the tables and chairs making a beeline right for me. I side stepped her but instead of her missing, she adjusted and tackled me like a fucking linebacker. The assholes outside of the room watching did nothing to help me. Then I saw him. Mick was standing on the other side of the glass with a shit-eating grin on his face. I suppose he thought that if he took me out like this, then nobody could say he did it. My friend was yelling at me to focus on the task at hand. I hadn't gotten a good look at her face at first, but as I fought her off and got on top of her to get th

e kill, my heart dropped. I was looking into the now, infected, Iz
zy. I was going to kill her, but instead, I took the syringe, and p
lunged it into her neck. She screamed and struggled for a minut
e or so, before finally succumbing to the drugs. The nurses rush
ed into the room and secured Izzy to the table she was on befor
e waking up. Mick was still looking in at me, I was so distraught,
that I walked out of the room, and went right for him. Unfortun
ately, he wasn't alone. I saw Josiah's smirking face right before t
he flash that comes with being hit in the head with the butt of an
assault rifle. Obviously, I'm not dead, and not being held captive
any more. Or I wouldn't be writing this. So don't worry for me jus
t yet. Anyways. I woke up in the interrogation room, AGAIN. This
time, Josiah was sitting in front of me, with the chair backwards,
arms crossed over the back rest. No smiles, no real emotion. Ju
st staring at me. I went to speak, but I couldn't due to the gag he
apparently affixed to my face. It tasted like shit. Like motor oil, a
nd other unspeakable shit. He told me he was going to remove t
he gag, and that if I so much as raised my voice, then he would
be forced to knock me back out again and wait for me to come t
o my senses. I nodded, to signify that I was going to be cooperat
ive. He went on to tell me that he and Mick had been watching
me. They were aware of what I was seeing as how they were th
ere when Dr. Stevens was interrogating me. I really didn't know
what to think at first. But as he spoke, I learned that he and Mick
were on to what she was up to. Mick apologized for his unfriendl
y demeanor, but he was trying to make it look like there was no
way that we would be able to get along with each other enough t

o do what they were going to propose. According to them, the la b team and Dr. Stevens had been grabbing random people that came here for sanctuary, and having some sort of “accident” tha t ends in them getting infected. So they can work on as fresh of a sample as they could get. They considered this the least risky way to do it. They claimed that they didn’t know that she was goi ng to do that to Izzy, or they would have intervened. What they wanted me to do, was to kill the good doctor and let them assum e control over the place. In turn, they would either make me part of their circle, or send me away, alive, depending on my ability t o do the job without being found out. Either way, I live to fight an other day. So, I had no choice but to agree. First we will need a plan.

32.

I started the whole process the way that I used to back before th e outbreak. It feels kind of good to be doing something I thoroug hly enjoyed again. All the others I killed after the outbreak were out of survival. This one however, feels like the old days. M y friend is absolutely ecstatic. “When do we get to finally kill this bitch!?” He screams with excitement. I shushed him, which didn’ t make a lot of sense when I think about it, it’s not as if any body can hear him, but sometimes, I am afraid someone will. He gets straight out deafening sometimes. Anyways, I got him to qu iet down so I could think.

I decided to do some recon before making any kind of moves. M ick got me a pass card to get through the security doors to the la b and the other restricted places. I haven't dared to even look in the room where they keep Izzy, I don't have time for the distracti on of emotion getting in the way. I still don't fully understand why I care about her. It's not as if I am attracted to her, she is a child after all, but, it's I guess comparable to how someone fe els about a younger sibling. I can't help but feel like I failed her and it sets a rage in me that will only feel better after I kill the person responsible. I still do not fully trust Josiah and Mick. Th ose two are shady as they come. There is a reason they made it to the level they did in this community. But nonetheless, they ar e providing me an outlet, a target, and the means to get it done with little to no concern of getting caught. Her routine is pretty st andard. She wakes up at 345am, turns on her coffee maker, tak es a shower which usually runs about 10-15 minutes, walks out of the bathroom after drying off, completely naked by the wa y, which is also how she sleeps, I have to admit, I had a hard ti me not getting aroused, but I stayed the course. She gets dres sed, eats breakfast, then leaves for work. I am not normally the kind of person that poisons someone to kill them. I like my kills t o be personal, and I like to watch the life leave in their eyes. The re is a sense of sick satisfaction I get from it. When I kill zombies , it's fun to me, but, there is no real joy in it. When you cave one of their heads in, it's not as if you get to watch the struggle leave their body, it's been long gone and replaced by something unint elligent, and that thinks of nothing else but the need to feed. Any ways, I thought briefly of killing her in her room, but, that would I ook entirely suspicious. I need to make this look like an accident. So, her place, is not the place to do it. I followed her for about 5 days before I knew what to do. I have it all planned out. Mick and Josiah want me to tell them what the plan is, but I am not going to tell them the actual plan just in case those two shifty eyed assholes double-cross me. Anyways. Wish me luck, I will be doing it tomorrow.

33.

I followed her. For the entirety of the day. It took so long to get to just the right moment. I waited until nobody was in the lab with her, snuck up behind her, and injected her with her own concoction she had used to infect Izzy. I felt it was the right thing to do, to make up for what she had done. The thing I didn't count on, was her telling me that the cure is complete and she needs me to administer it to Izzy. She also asked me, that if it indeed works, that she would like me to use it on her, and then she was planning on sending myself and Izzy to the CDC in Georgia to mass produce it. Apparently there is a military entity protecting the facility to ensure the scientists inside are able to continue working on a cure. I did what was asked of me regardless of what my friend felt, regardless of what Mick and Josiah wanted. They were right, she was a horrible person, but at the same time, I can't rea lly judge her for what she was. Just as she could no longer judg e me. The evil we are, is necessary for the surviving what the world has turned into. If I believed in a god, I would think that thi s was the purpose I was created for. She went on to tell me that Mick was indeed immune to the disease and the cure was deri ved from his DNA and they needed a freshly infected specimen t o create the cure. In theory, as long as the subject is not at the " rotting" stage, they can be cured. It is especially useful to those who were freshly infected. I went into the room where Izzy was k ept and the room was kept extremely cold. I suppose that was d one to keep her from deteriorating. I'm not really sure. I'm not a doctor, or a scientist. Just a person doing what they think needs to be done. Anyways, she was tied down on the gurney. I look ed her in the eyes as I went to inject her with the cure. It was the strangest thing to watch. I watched as the life returned to her ey es and the intelligence came back. I have watched the life leav e so many people's eyes as I killed them, but never have I seen it in reverse. It was beautiful poetry. My friend was even awestri cken and happy to see her come back. "Oh goody!! I liked her!!" he exclaimed with the giddiness that usually came with watching me dispatch someone. It was kind of un-nerving to be honest. I never really like it when he's happy, because that means he got his way. Well, whatever. Izzy was back, and she seemed to be herself. I then went back to Dr. Stevens to give her the cure as well, but that's where the plan was unfortunately for her, change d. As I walked into the lab, Izzy stayed close behind me, and

we could hear the growl of a zombie and shouting. I crept up to
the door where I left the doctor, and looked in. Josiah had her h
eld from behind, and Mick was hitting her in the head with a ha
mmer. To their dismay, she was not dying. Somehow, the only t
hing being damaged, was her flesh on her head where blood w
as shooting out profusely. Somehow, she was still standing and
trying to break free to kill her attackers. I don't know why this ma
de me angry. The whole time planning this out, I had no intentio
ns to leave her alive, but, again with these stupid feelings and
thoughts I have had lately. I feel so conflicted sometimes. I walk
ed into the room, and instantly, they were both distracted by
me coming in the room. So distracted that Dr. Stevens was a
ble to break free and rip Micks throat out. Josiah, reeling from w
hat had just happened, ran from the room. That's when she turn
ed her attention to me. I wanted to help her, so, perhaps out of s
tupidity, or something else, I don't really understand, I ran strai
ght at her and tackled her to the ground. In the process, she tore
a chunk out of my right forearm. I managed to inject her with the
remainder of the cure. Izzy helped me to keep her subdued unt
il she was back to normal. The problem then was that she was
no longer unaffected by her wounds. I really wished at that mom
ent that I was not so stupid. As she laid dying in my arms, she to
ld me, I either have an hour or so to live, or I have nothing to
worry about from the bite. The infection is not all dooming. Som
e people have been made stronger by it, some have been compl
etely unaffected, and others, well, we have been dealing with th
em since the onset of this epidemic. She told myself and Izzy t

o go into her office and open her safe. She gave us the code, and instructed me to make sure Izzy gets out alive and heads directly to the CDC. She would have had us take Mick, but he laid dead on the ground next to her. She said that Izzy has the cure in her blood and will be able to supply the CDC with what is needed along with the formula in the safe, to recreate the cure. There is a long drive ahead of her, and I am unsure whether or not I am going to live through this. I have instructed Izzy to kill me if I start to change or act crazier than normal much to the displeasure of my friend. If I die, he dies. He is not very happy about the situation at all. If this is my last entry, then so be it. I hope she makes it, I hope humanity gets another chance, and I would apologize for what I have done with my life, but I am not really sorry. If there is a hell where I'm going, I hope I burn well! Otherwise, wish me luck. – J

Chapter 8 – Izzy

40.

My name is Izzy. I am 13 years old. I have no idea what I am su pposed to do here. Johnny is not dead. However, he is changing . I have strapped him down in the back of the cargo truck I'm dri ving. I was fortunate enough to get the help of Josiah and anoth er person named Jerome to get him into the vehicle and strappe d down so if I can get there fast enough, and get a cure made. Maybe I can get him back like he did for me. I know he's not a "g ood" person, but he has saved me more than once. He has don e more for me than anyone else has ever done. I will not fail him , and I will get this formula to the CDC. I have MREs and weapo ns with lots of ammo, and lots of full fuel cans strapped down in the back as well. I will be as safe as possible and will continue t o write in his journal until he is back. I hope.

41.

Well, so far so good. I found an abandoned hotel to stay in over night. Johnny isn't making enough noise to attract attention. I had a difficult time getting him into the room seeing as how they tied him up just in case he fully turns before we get to where we're going. I am half his size so this was a pain in the ass to do. Firstly, before I could get him into a room, I needed a key, which was of course in the front of the hotel, in the lobby, which was locked and boarded up, but I saw a window open for a room above the entrance, so I scaled the building using one of the drainage pipes to get to the floor, then I had to shimmy my way to the window. So much fun. When I got into the room, it was dark, and smelled of death. I had brought a crow-bar with me in case I ran into anything while I was there. Fortunately, there was nothing but dead, not moving bodies in the room. I snuck passed them as if one false move would have woken them up. Honestly, I have seen too many times where I thought they were dead, and almost ended up lunch. So I don't trust a damn thing. I got down to the first floor after carefully sneaking through the halls and down the stairs. There doesn't seem to be anything lurking about here. Kind of pleasantly surprised. Anyways, we got a room on the ground floor since I can't really carry him. Hopefully, we'll get some rest, and move on as soon as we wake up. Johnny doesn't look like he is changing very fast, but it is obvious that he *is* changing. It's weird how some people change right away, and others seem to resist longer. I'll never fully understand.

42.

So...... Where to begin? Johnny, after pretty much being inactiv e and quiet, picks the night where I need the quiet the most, t o break his silence and start screaming bloody fucking murder f or what seemed like fifteen fucking minutes! Every god-damn ed dead thing in the area heard it and we had to vacate the pre mises like NOW. So, that's what we did. Thankfully, he wasn't p articularly active, aside from the screaming. So, getting him into the vehicle and getting what's called the fuck out of there, was not really too hard. I will chalk it up to the adrenaline that an enc ounter that could end in death, dismemberment, and the possi bility of becoming one of those damn thing causes, being the re ason that I had the strength to do it. I don't know how he did th is alone for as long as he did. Aside from the not having to carry a semi-dead person strapped to a cot on wheels, this shit sucks. Being alone in general sucks. To have someone just to talk to, that talks back, would be fantastic... Instead, I get the occasiona l grunts and moans from Johnny and of course the screaming. I have been sorely tempted to tape his mouth shut to silence it to at least muffled screaming, but I can't bring myself to do it at the moment. I know for sure I am not going to try the hotel thing aga in. So, maybe I will find a quiet area, lock the vehicle down, an d get rest wherever and whenever I can. I have quite a while to go, so the less I stop, the faster I should get there. Goodbye fo r now.

43.

I dreamt last night that I was home. Not with the dickhead around, but with my mom. We were dressed like the people you see in those wholesome family shows where there is no such thing as crime and conflict. We were eating breakfast at the table together and talking about me joining the cheerleader squad. I laughed myself awake at the thought of this only to be looking at a zombie, face to face. He we looking at me through the window on the driver side door. There weren't seemingly any others around, so I grabbed my crowbar, kicked the door open hard, which made him fall to the ground, jumped out of the truck and impaled his head with the pointy end. After that I gathered a few sticks and made a small fire. I ate an MRE and drank some haphazardly made hot cocoa that came with the meal, and cleaned up a bit with what was left of the water I boiled. I really miss showers and soap. Now all I smell is myself. I suppose I smell way worse than I think, seeing as how you just kind of get so used to it, that you don't smell it anymore, but every now and then, I smell it, and it is not even remotely pleasant. I miss that, and TV. I hope someday this all goes back to normal.

44.

I am at a loss. I feel like this nightmare should end but, it hasn't.

I'm so sick of driving, sleeping, driving....... This is bullshit. I hate being alive sometimes. I really have contemplated just givi ng up. Johnny has been nothing but silent for the last few day s, which oddly hasn't helped me any. At this point, I welcome t he grunting and screaming he was doing. I have about 150 mile s to go before I should make it to the CDC. I bet there is not hing there. I bet we went this whole fucking way, just to find no thing but rotting, walking, biting corpses. FUCK this shit! FUCK YOU! FUCK YOU! FUCK YOU! Why the fuck am I even writing i n this damn thing? Johnny was. It's not like he's some important part of history is it? I am just taking him with me in hopes we can cure him and get back to surviving. I bet there isn't shit there... ... And then I'll have to kill him, to put him out of his misery, and out of mine. Ugh......

45.

I was wrong for once. There are people there. So that's the goo d news. The bad news is that it's heavily guarded and they seem to shoot first, and ask questions afterward. I watched the m gun three people down in front of the entry point. I couldn't tell what happened because I was far away with binoculars, but I need to be very cautious how I do this. They may just start firin g right away as I pull up, or they might kill Johnny before I get to explain what we're doing here. I really hope this goes right for o nce. If I don't write anymore, I'm dead... Wish me luck. Great, n ow I'm talking to the damn thing like it's a person, and not just a journal. Whatever.

Chapter 9 – Aftermath

46.

So, I have made it in one piece. At first, the guys at the gate wer e going to shoot Johnny, but I was able to talk some sense int o him, if that’s what you call talking someone out of shooting wh at appears to be a zombie. But it’s whatever. I got to the gate an d was met with commands from the roof to exit the vehicle slowl y, and keep my hands up. I explained that I had something they would be interested in assuming this is still a facility being used for research and not a base being used for survival only. They a ssured me that most of the scientists are very much still alive and working on a cure. Or at least a vaccine for this epidemic. After we finally got in, they removed Johnny from his restraints and moved him to a cell for his, and their protection. He really didn't react to any of it, as if he were in a sort of dream state. The doctor, Reinfeld, was his name. Was extremely excited to see what I had brought with me all this way. He said he had his theories on what would pass for a cure, but could never quite find the right ratios. Which kind of struck me as odd seeing as how he was old as dirt and seemed to be in his field of research for his entire life. I base this off of all the big words he threw around. I won't even pretend to understand even half of it. He told me that with this formula and a few more tests, he could easily recreate and mass produce it with little time. He asked if I would mind him using Johnny in the tests for the cure. With the assurance that no harm would come to him unless it was completely necessary, and by my hand, I reluctantly agreed. I'm hoping he doesn't get upset if he comes around and reads this. Sorry Johnny. I hope this works though. You may have been a monster at one time, but now you can be a savior. Thank you for saving my life several times, and thank you for being like a brother to me. I probably wouldn't still be here if it weren't for you.

47.

Doctor Reinfeld came to me today to show me his progress. He said that he knows I'm not a scientist, but because I came here with the formula, he felt compelled to share whatever breakthrou ghs he makes. He had a zombie captured in the observation r oom a couple cells down from Johnny. He had me watch as thre e men in leather and stainless steel armor walked into the room, two of them held it, while the third injected it with something. Th e zombie instantly fell to the floor, screaming, and after what fel t like twenty minutes, it laid still. I turned to walk away, but the d octor insisted I stay and watch what happens. After another cou ple minutes, the zombie sat up and started screaming again, onl y instead of screaming like a zombie, I could understand what it was saying. It was a woman's voice. She begged for death. S he was in pain from the decomposition and was not able to com prehend why she was alive and in such pain. The doctor nodded to the others to put her out of her misery. He was obviously plea sed with himself. And I couldn't blame him, though, I was unhap py with the fact that she suffered the way she did. He said he wasn't going to use this strain on Johnny. He wanted to use som ething that would help him to heal and not be in so much pain w hen he wakes up. “It should only take a couple more days and we’ll be ready.” He promised. We will see.

48.

I woke up to a conversation between two guys a couple bunks d own from me. They were not all too pleased with the doctor sh owing me so much attention and never letting other people in th e group that have been there longer, see any of his work. “Al ong comes this little cunt, and the “good doctor” has to let her in on everything. We should cut this little bitch down to size Her, a nd her fucking pet. It’s not like he’s not already all but changed. We would be doing them both a favor, and ourselves. Let’s kill h er tomorrow. I’ll need a day to plan out disposal and whatnot.” I can’t say I don’t understand the way they feel, but I’m not letting this happen to either of us. They think they’ll be taking out a little defenseless girl, but they don’t have any fucking idea what they’ re messing with. They’ll find out. And we will leave this place aft er the doc gives the dose to Johnny. I’m not staying any longer t han that. I will let the doctor know that tomorrow, of course, AFT ER he treats Johnny.

49.

Well, the cure worked…. But I don't think Johnny will be OK for a while. The "cure" the doctor gave to him, didn't work like the others. It brought him back to being cognitive, and all of his memory seems to be there. But there is something off with him now. He talks to me and other people like normal, but he is now arguing and I mean intensely arguing with another person that isn't actually there. From some of the things he says, nothing the other is saying, is really good. I told Johnny that we needed to leave, and he agreed to come with me. But as soon as I turned my back, he was talking to his imaginary friend. "No, I don't know how we got here! Shut the fuck up and let me think! And no, we aren't fucking killing anyone right now!" I'm not sure what's happened to him, but, it's probably not good. He says we leave in about an hour. I'm happy to have him back, but I hope he's not going to lose his shit and kill me, or anyone else that doesn't need to die.

50.

Annnnnnnnd I'm officially freaked out. We got to the truck, and we were getting in, when the guys that were talking about killing us showed up. Johnny was way too calm at first. Telling them that there was no reason to do anything to us because we were leaving and there is no reason they should throw their lives away. To which they laughed and one of them brandished a large

military knife. Like the ones you see attached to a rifle in the old
war movies. The guy who pulled out the knife, stabbed him right
in the chest! But Johnny didn't even seem bothered by it. He act
ually smiled at the asshole, pulled the knife out, stabbed him rep
eatedly while his friend watched in horror and disbelief, then he
turned his head and asked "What should we do with this fuck? A
re you sure? Okay, I think we can do that" he walked towards th
e other man, who was now pale as the moon itself, and tore his t
hroat out with one fluid motion. It was unreal, terrifying, and som
ehow, kind of cool to watch to be completely honest. Whatever it
is that the doctor injected him with, brought him back, but not wit
hout side effects, if you want to call them that. I am really hopefu
l that this doesn't end with me being on the receiving end of one
of these episodes. I am going to be extra careful around him unti
l I fully understand what it is that I'm actually dealing with. I am
very curious to know what he means by "We". I'm very sure it w
asn't me he was talking to, but there was nobody next to him wh
en he said it. I'm a little bit un-easy to say the least. Hopefully th
is is nothing to worry about. I don't think he would do anything to
me, it's not like he hasn't had the chance to, but this makes me i
ncredibly uneasy.

Chapter 10 – Johnny's Triumphant Return?

51.

I feel like shit. My mouth always tastes like rot and my breath do esn't smell any better. I keep having these dreams of eating. Bu t I'm not eating food. I'm eating the corpses of dead zombies. I d on't have really good dreams in general, but, this is just disgusti ng. What's worse about these dreams is that I don't dislike the taste of their flesh. I of course have no idea what zombie flesh ta stes like, but, in my dreams, it's like eating something completel y delicious like ice cream, or banana pudding. Not that it tastes like that in my dream, but when you think of things that are pleas ant to eat, that's what I think of. It doesn't stink, it is warm, and j uicy. Every greedy bite I take is better than the last and I just ca n't stop myself. My mind reels in horror, but my body keeps takin g more and more greedy, sloppy bites of dead flesh. At some p oint during my dream, I could hear a cackling laughter coming fr om behind me. It's my friend. He has this sickening smile on his face and he tells me to go back to enjoying my "little snack". I o f course for some reason, do as he say with no hesitation. I don' t know what to make of it, but it really doesn't make me all too c

omfortable. I would share my dream with Izzy, but she has spok
en very little to me since the incident outside of the CDC. I don't
know where that strength came really came from. I can only ass
ume that it has something to do with the "Cure" they injected me
with. From what I have seen so far, this disease or whatever it is
, really doesn't react the same in every person. Some people t
urn into straight out zombies, some just seem completely unaffe
cted by it, and then others just die. I feel different. My skin seem
s to be changing in color to a more grayish-green. My nails hav
e gone black. My teeth seem sharper, though they don't look lik
e it in the mirror, they feel like they have gotten sharper. My eye
s are bloodshot to the point where the whites of my eyes are a
deep, dark, crimson color. My head hurts constantly and I am ex
tremely hungry. Fortunately, human flesh isn't at all appetizing t
o me. So I guess I have that going for me. Nothing I eat seems t
o want to stay down permanently either. I just end up puking it b
ack up with a bunch of cold black shit. I just feel hunger, and
pain. My sense of smell is a bit off too. Nothing smells appetizin
g. Nothing smells bad. I can't smell anything at all. I'm hoping
this passes, but I'm starting to think it's going to be like this for
me from now on. We are going to be on the road for a while acc
ording to Izzy. We have no real destination at the moment, bu
t she seems determined to just keep driving for as long as we ca
n without stopping. I'm going to sleep for a bit to pass the time.

52.

I was awakened to a huge bump followed by cursing, and a loud
bang from the right-rear tire. The tire exploded and we were forc
ed to stop the vehicle. Unfortunately, we don't have a fucking sp
are or equipment to change the damn tire. We don't really see
m like we are close to anything helpful either. So, we're going to
have to hoof it for a while until we at least find somewhere safe t
o regroup and come up with a plan. We grabbed our backpac
ks, loaded them with as much food and water as we could phy
sically carry. Naturally, I'm carrying the most, because equality a
nd shit lol! I can't believe the fucking luck we're having, but I g
uess it's way better than being dead. My friend was kind enough
to bring my attention to the big group of dead fucks walking towa
rds the vehicle from out of the woods and the storm rolling in fro
m the distance. We need to get our asses out of here so it's goo
dbye until we find somewhere better to be. Wish us luck.

53.

We are safe and sound in a storm shelter for now. At least as far
as we can tell. The horde was quite a bit slower than we were a

nd we seemed to have given them the slip, however, the weather was not so slow. It was just getting on top of us and we spotted a tornado forming as we came up on this old deserted farmhouse. It didn't look sturdy enough for us to hide in the house for shelter and we weren't about to try to clear the house of unknown threats amidst a nasty storm. We were fortunate to spot the storm shelter in the back yard so we got our asses into safety. There isn't too much down here. A couple cases of bottled water, cans of ravioli and other old cans of veggies and cured meat. There was even some old porno mags and a broken radio. We used the candles we found in the corner so we didn't have to use our batteries up with our flashlights. We're going to get some sleep and check things out in the morning.

54.

I was dreaming about eating zombies again, or so I thought. Unfortunately that wasn't the case. A couple of them found us and opened the door to the storm shelter while we were asleep and went right for me. One of them bit me on the forearm. I forced my arm into their mouth with enough force to dislocate its jaw. I then grabbed its mouth and snapped it all the way open. This not only ripped its jaw from its face, but also partially decapitated it. I then turned my attention to Izzy who was screaming for help as one of them was on top of her and very much overpowering her. I kicked him in the ribs hard enough where I felt his ribs crack an d he went flying into the wall behind Izzy. I then got on top of hi m and before I knew what was happening, I took a bite out of his neck. The warm puss oozed out of the wound and only made me crazier. I was not in control of myself anymore. I just kept biti ng, chewing, and swallowing chunks of his putrid, rotting flesh. It was so good. I couldn't get seem to get enough. After he quit twi tching, I turned to the one that bit me earlier and ate chunks off of it as well. I say it, because I really couldn't tell if it was a he, or a she. After my appetite was satiated, I couldn't help but not ice Izzy in the corner, crying. I tried to comfort her, and tell her al l was ok now and we were safe, but when I went to put a hand on her shoulder, she screamed at me to "get the fuck away" f rom her. I just walked to the entrance, opened the door, and we nt out to see what had happened in the storm. My friend, look ed at me with his usual shitty grin, and laughed. I told him I w asn't in the mood for his shit right now, and he stopped smiling. " THIS ISN'T A TIME FOR YOU TO START ACTING LIKE A LITT LE BITCH JOHNNY!" "I finally know how we can co-exist!" I gav e him a dirty look but kept listening. (As if I really had much of a choice.) "You can be Johnny. Normal, boring as fuck, Johnny. I'll be the one who controls the killing and eating of these walking di nner specials!" It seems to me, that you're too conflicted about it , and I'm assuming you find it pretty disgusting, so why not relin quish your control to me for the un-pleasantries?" I told him und er one condition would I ever consider such a “deal”. He is not to hurt people unless I agree. The undead however, are fair game. Also, he isn’t allowed full control at any time. I need to be able to stop him if he gets out of control. He agreed to my terms, so I agreed to his. The question I have in this is, what sense does it make, that I’m making deals with something that is supposedly just in my head as my old shrink used to tell me. I shouldn’t be doing this probably, but again, I don’t see much of a choice. I wish I really knew what in the fuck this guy really is. I may be crazy, but you never hear about someone making deals with their other personality, or imaginary friend, do you? I don’t know what to make of it. Also, if he is just a figment of my imagination, why doesn’t he disappear when I tell him to go away? Why can’t I read his thoughts, or control him in any way? And why can’t he read my mind for that matter? Or can he and he isn’t saying anything? FUCK.... I don’t know, and this is giving me a damn migraine. Fuck it.

Chapter 11 – Lost

55.

“This is Izzy. I’m leaving and I don’t want you to come looking for me. I’m not mad at you so much as I am extremely terrified of y ou. Please don't feel like this is something you caused, though it is a bit, I don't blame you. You don't seem like you can control what you are, or what you do. Just go your way, and I'll go mine. If we do happen to cross paths again, I won't turn on you, but I won't go with you. I am going to find another group if I can, to survive this life we were given, in this world we were unfortunate enough to be stuck in. I miss normalcy and will hopefully find it. Please take care of yourself. Help others you run across. I think that is your purpose, but I am not OK with watching you do any of the things I've seen you do anymore. I am sorry, and I am grateful for the help you've given me, several times, even before all of this. When you killed my stepdad, when you got me cured, I owe you for everything, but I can't do this. Thanks Johnny. – Izzy"

56.

So, here I am alone. She left me here while I wasn't paying attention. I found some canned peaches in the kitchen, along with some cigarettes and drink mix pouches. But when I got to the shelter, she was gone. For the first time, I felt sadness. Real sadness. She was my friend. She was a good kid. I don't blame her for running, it must have been horrible to watch. I really wish she would have waited until were somewhere safe though. Fuck it. I'm going to follow her if I can find her trail, and watch over her at least until she manages to get somewhere safe.

57.

I went onto the roof and looked around for a bit. As I was about t o give up, I heard a scream off in the distance in the woods. I'm going to go investigate. I hope I'm not too late.

58.

I went to where I heard the screaming, but I found nothing but z ombies, I'm sure that she came this way because she dropped her knife. But I can't find her. The trail has seemingly gone cold. I guess I'm on my own for now. It's not like I haven't been befo re and it's not like I'm not a whole hell of a lot stronger than I wa s before I got infected. I don't much like the side effects though. I'm starting to have physical changes. I have noticed, that my ski n is dry and cracking in places, not all over, but on my elbows, knees, knuckles, neck, and the corners of my mouth. The whites of my eyes seem to be yellowing, with bits of dark red. I don 't know what to think of it, but I'm obviously concerned about my health. It's not like I can just go see a doctor, so I hope for the b est... I'm exhausted to the point I that I can't continue, so I am g oing to get some rest and try to find her in the morning. Goodnig ht.

59.

I was awakened in the middle of the night by screaming and a lo t of noise. It sounded like gun fire. I ran out to the roof to investi gate, and I could see a large truck with about ten people around it. They were all shooting in one direction. The zombies that we re scattered around the house I have been in, were suddenly, ve ry interested in the noise. So they walked out to investigate. They got three of them before the rest noticed, and panic ensued. The rest got in the truck and took off like a bat out of hell, but unfortunately crashed into the ditch. Two of them took off towards a nearby barn and shut the doors. I continued to watch. The three that were swarmed, are completely gone from what I can see. There hasn't been any motion from the truck for a good ten minutes, and the zombies are pretty much completely occupied with trying to get into that barn, so I figure I'll go ahead and try my luck with checking the truck for survivors, gear, and food, whatever I can get. I know it sounds shitty, but what they can't use (since they're dead), I can.

60.

I crept up to the truck, being careful not to make any noise and bring attention to myself. Upon looking in the truck, it seemed that everyone was definitely dead. So I started grabbing their bags, I found a couple hand guns, MREs, and there was a box of ammo, and flares. I continued looking for a minute, and noticed another military type metal box. I opened it, and found it was full of grenades. Hmmmm, I thought to myself, these could definitely prove to be useful. So I took a few trips to get everything. But on the last trip, one of the people in the truck, woke up. He looked at me, grabbed his flash light and pointed it directly at my face. I didn't notice he had a gun. He shot at me, and I thought he missed. I quickly subdued him, but when I wrestled the gun from his hand, he had a grenade and pulled the pin. I got out of the tru

ck just on time to at least get missed by all the shrapnel. That no
ise brought the attention of ALL of the damn zombies in the area
. They were upon me before I could even get my shit togethe
r from the blast. My ears were ringing, and my vision was blurry.
By the time I was back to full capacity, they were everywhere. B
ut something strange happened. They weren't at all interested i
n me. I was panicked at first, but they just walked past me like I
was not even there. I even pushed one of them and shouted at i
t, but, nothing, not even a glance. Unless this is somehow just a
freak occurrence, that means, I don't have to hide from them.
I will try to test this out later. Meanwhile. I got my ass back in the
house. I went into the bathroom, to wash up, and when I took off
my shirt, I looked in the mirror. I actually got hit when he shot at
me. But, I wasn't bleeding. There was just a hole, and the flesh
around the wound, was discolored. I stuck my finger in and felt n
o pain. I think I am one of them. But why do I have cognitive th
ought? Why can I speak clearly? I'm so hungry..... I need to eat.
But food makes me sick. I need to eat......

61.

I woke up out in the woods. I was covered in what I can describe
as zombie guts. I ate again. There were the half eaten corpses
of at least three zombies from what I could tell. They don't stink t
o me, which is weird. They almost smell, sweet. Like freshly ba
ked cookies. But, I digress. I walked back to house. I was weari
ng nothing but my underwear, so I needed to get dressed. I wen
t into the bathroom and grabbed my journal, and the clothes I se

emingly decided to just take off. And went to get myself dressed. I noticed that my shirt was just covered in blood, and other unide ntifiable shit. My pants were pretty jacked up too. So I went thro ugh the bags I managed to take from the truck. I found some old brown pants, they were clean, and a white t-shirt in one of them. I found fresh underwear and socks in another, and an olive dra b military style jacket. It was obviously expensive at one point w hen that sort of jacket was in style. It was definitely not the real thing, too thin. But either way, it was nice to put on clean clothes , even though, I haven't showered in a while. I couldn't smell my self, so I assume I stink, but not that bad, and who would I be i mpressing anyways right?! Anyways, I need to go, find a vehicl e, and come back here to get this stuff I found in the truck. It's fa r too useful to leave behind. I think I'll bring one of the guns wit h me, empty one of the bags out, and pack some water, and foo d in case I need to help anyone, and check the barn while I'm at it. Wish me luck.

62.

I decided to investigate the barn before looking for a vehicle. Mo st of the zombies had cleared out, I only had to kill a couple of t hem before approaching the front doors. They had been secure d from the inside and I could hear whispering. They were trying t o figure out who was creeping around outside. I decided to spea k to them. I told them I wasn't there to hurt them and that it was safe to come out as long as they were quiet about it. As soon a s they saw me, they freaked out. Apparently I look worse than I

originally thought. Fortunately they weren't armed with guns, just
melee type weapons, a bat and a crowbar. So, when they tried
to be threatening, I pointed my gun at them and told them to go
about their business and to forget we met. I did let them know all
of their friends were dead, and that the vehicle and all the gear i
n it other than the bag of clothes were destroyed. I could tell the
y didn't completely believe me about the gear, but they definitel
y believed I would shoot them dead if they were to stay any lo
nger. So they left. I watched them walk away until they complete
ly disappeared over the horizon, then I went back to the hous
e and set up a couple traps so if they were to get any stupid id
eas about breaking into the house to reclaim their plundered ge
ar, they wouldn't make it out alive. I then decided to take advant
age of having pretty much a full day of sunlight to work with and
go find a vehicle. After walking for what seemed like four or five
miles, I ran across a gas station. I had to dispatch a couple of d
ead asses in the store, and picked up a few things. I really want
ed a cigarette so I grabbed a pack from behind the register. I fin
d it funny that money is now completely useless in this world. Ev
eryone was so enslaved by money, that it was hard to fathom a
world without it. Humans are so fucking stupid. We wasted our g
ifts on consumerism when we should have been more worried a
bout prolonging our lives, improving our lives in the sense of qua
lity of life, not how much shit we can buy. What video games w
e can get, what movies are coming out, what's the newest rage i
n the fucking fashion, what the celebrities are doing, wearing,
who their fucking, and all this other menial bullshit. I never real

ly fell into that shit, but I of course couldn't deny the need to make money before all of this happened. It's been so long since I had my medication that I kind of can't imagine what it would be like if I was still on it. This new world is more suited for the insane. People who don't have a moral compass will survive longer than your "good" people. Everyone who is alive today has done some fucked up shit to survive. So even the good are bad.

63.

The gas station was a wash, so I left after grabbing a warm ass soda and some smokes. I know it's not healthy, but, I am starting to think that any health problems from smoking and eating unhealthy are the least of my health problems based off of the fact I am still not bleeding or feeling any pain from being shot earlier. Yay evolution?? Whatever, I'm still mentally here, so, I'm going to continue collecting resources, and hopefully, I'll find Izzy before anything bad happens to her. I'll keep you posted. Not that you're really reading this lol! Why am I still writing in this thing? Oh yeah. So I can keep a little of my sanity..... Or some shit like that...

64.

I continued walking for another couple hours and I came across a long driveway leading into the woods. After walking down it for a while, I found the garage. There was a really nice, antique Dodge Challenger. It looks like it's probably about late 70's. I'm not really all too sure, since I am not a big car person. I was al

ways better with computers and other electronics. It seems like
kind of a useless thing to have knowledge in anymore. But it is
what it is. I checked the oil, and gas, it seems fine, so I will use it
. I went into the house to see if there was anything useful. I foun
d a bunch of canned goods, a carton of cigarettes, candles, flare
s, and clothes. They had running water and soap in the bathroo
m. The electricity didn't work, nor did the gas, so it was a cold sh
ower, not that I minded. It was nice to get clean and put on clea
n clothes. I looked around the house while brushing my teeth wit
h one of the tooth brushes I found. Again, I don't think health pro
blems are a thing I need to worry about anymore, and I finally fo
und where the family had gone too. In the basement, they were
neatly lined up, hung, and it looked like they were skinned and b
led dry. On the wall behind them, there was something writte
n in their blood. "Repent Sinners! The End Is Nigh!" Fucking reli
gious nuts. What point is there to committing a murder of an en
tire family, in the name of your religion? Then you write some du
mb shit like that on the wall behind them? Aren't you, yourself c
ommitting a "Sin"? Ugh, people are so fucking stupid. Whatever,
their loss I suppose. I don't know what really possessed me to d
o it, maybe it was the fact that one of them was very small. I cou
ldn't tell what gender they were, or who was who, but I felt comp
elled to cut them down, and I took them outside and buried their
bodies. Humanity is a thing that sometimes was beautiful, other
times, ugly. I sometimes miss things being "normal", but that
kind of thing, isn't a good survival tactic anymore. After I buried t
hem, I packed the stuff I found in the house, and headed back to

where I had my other stuff. I packed that into the car, and heade
d out looking for signs of where Izzy could have gone too. I think
it's worth mentioning that my traps were still in place, so that m
eans nobody ended up trying to steal my shit lol! Bye for now.

65.

I drove for about an hour when I saw what looked like the flash f
rom gun fire in the distance. I killed my headlights and drove sl
owly with the windows down. I could hear shouting when I got cl
oser and the screams and growls of what sounded like hundre
ds of zombies. I took out my binoculars and tried to look, but
the sun was down too far and I couldn't really make anything out
. I drove closer and then stashed the car where it wouldn't easil
y be seen. I took the keys out of the car and locked it so if anyo
ne did happen to stumble upon it, they wouldn't be making off wi
th it. I crept into the field where near the gates of this textile fact
ory where it looked like there were about five people shooting at
anything that got close enough to harm them, while a sixth pers
on was trying with all they had, to get into the building through t
he door. I ran back to the car and grabbed some of my flares. I a
lso grabbed a few grenades and the shotgun. I walked up to the
driveway of the factory and started shouting. Some of the de
adies stopped and looked at me, then went back to what they w
ere doing. So, I lit a flare, and popped a round into the sky. Th
is, go their attention. I dropped the flare and reeled back. When
a good amount of them surrounded the flare, I threw a grenade.
This killed pretty much all but maybe ten of them. I then, went in

to the midst of the zombies and butt stroked, shot, and beat them until they were all dead. That's when the hunger kicked in. I blacked out. It was like a dream. All of a sudden, I was at some buffet place. There were fat people, everywhere, all lined up with their trays, and their plates, taking from the buffet line. But there wasn't food that you would find in a restaurant, just rotting corpses. They were taking huge, glopping, servings of these rotting corpses, and sitting down at their tables, and greedily chowing down. I was almost sickened by the sight, until the smell hit me. Like a sweet smell of freshly baked brownies, or pie, or even fresh barbeque. I gravitated to the line. I didn't have a tray, so I just started grabbing greedy handfuls and eating, and eating, and eating. It was at this moment of bliss that one of the customers started screaming at me. "What the fuck are you?!?" The rest started screaming incoherently. And I awoke. I was strapped into a chair, in what I could only think at the time, would be the managerial office of the factory they were trying to gain access to. I thought to myself as I woke up and realized that I was in restraints, I really should learn to mind my own fucking business. My friend was there. Staring at me, looking, for once, a bit concerned. "What have you gotten us into friend of mine?" He said to me, still looking very worried. That was when a rather large man stepped into the room, accompanied by two other, less large men. They didn't say anything to me, or to each other, they just stood there. Looking at me, as if studying and trying to comprehend what exactly it was they were looking at. The smallest of the three men, then walked calmly out of the office and sh outed for someone named Bella. He then came back into the room and took his place next to the others. I could hear her footsteps. I had guessed she wasn't a very big person based off of how they sounded, but I was wrong. She was a very heavyset, but not exactly what I would call fat, woman. She looked like one of those body-builder women you would see occasionally in a magazine, or on the internet. Just fucking huge. She asked me one question, "What are you?" I didn't know how to answer the question, because I don't really know what I am. So, when I didn't answer, she nodded to the guys that came in before her, and two of them held me, and of course, the big asshole, would hit me. She asked again. I then answered, "I don't know". She didn't much like that answer, so they hit me again. This went on for a while. The funny thing, is that it didn't hurt. I didn't really bleed, but I did spit out chunks of black shit, and some half chewed zombie flesh I was unaware was in my mouth at the time. I finally got pissed and screamed at her. "I don't know what the fuck I am! But if you don't stop this shit, you will fucking find out!" She didn't really seem to be at all frightened of this threat, and nodded to the big asshole again, only this time, he didn't get to hit me. Instead, my friend said "My turn!" and my body was seemingly out of my control. Though I didn't feel the urge to stop what was happening either. My arms broke free of the restraints, I grabbed the guy on my right, yanked him down to my mouth, and tore a chunk out of his neck. He fell to the ground screaming. The guy on my left let go and ran out of the room yelling. This big asshole in front of me, tried to put me back into the chair to tie me ba ck down, but failed miserably when my left hand found his throat , and tore his Adams apple out. I rose from my chair and started towards her when I heard someone in the background scream. “Stop! I know him, and he’s not dangerous if you don’t attack him! Please stop!” The voice was familiar. And soon I found out why. As I stared at Bella, the door to the office opened. “Johnn y! Sit down and relax please!” It was Izzy. I felt a great relief, an d regained full control of myself. She told them I was her frie nd and, that regardless of my appearance, I am only a threat wh en I need to be. She told me she was sorry for running off and th at she wouldn’t leave me again. She was just not ready to see w hat I had become and freaked out. I kind of don’t blame her. I have become what seems, a bit of a monster. I thought I was ba d before, but now…. I am literally a monster. Thankfully, I gue ss, I still have thought, intelligent thought. I still have emotion. I s till can think for myself and communicate. I apologized to the gro up for killing their friends, which, of course, they didn’t really see m to be forgiving about. Which is why they told me to leave. Izzy tried to get them to understand that I only did what I did in self-d efense. They, understandably, did not feel it necessary to hear h er out, and kicked her out as well. I have apologized to Izzy sev eral times, and she says I don’t need to be sorry, but I am. I r eally don’t understand what I am, and I don’t much like what I ha ve become. I can’t eat regular food. I can drink all the soda, wat er, or beer I want, that doesn’t make me sick, but real food, that makes me sick beyond belief. I can only eat flesh. Dead flesh… … I even puked up the chunk of flesh I took out of that guy in th e factory. So, no live flesh, no real food, just putrid, rotting, dead, fucking flesh. I can’t really complain as it at least tastes and smells good to me, but my still very functional brain, does not like the look or thought of consuming zombie meat. Izzy tells me, we’ll be OK. Hopefully, she’s right.

Chapter 12 – Found

66.

My dreams, are of horrible things now. It’s not like I had good dreams before, but now, my current life is leaking into my nightmares. I had a dream I haven’t had in a long time. The one I talked about long before this zombie thing happened and society fell. The dream where my stepdad killed my mother in front of me when I was a child. Only this time, there were differences. One, it wasn’t my mom that got killed, it was Izzy, two, it wasn’t my stepdad, at least not like I knew him. It was a zombie version of him, and instead of cutting her throat with a kitchen knife, he bit her neck and blood sprayed all over his face, he somehow managed to laugh though. And I wasn’t a child, but a monster. A hulking thing with black claws, and spikes protruding from my spine, elbows, and knees. I was wearing pants, but they were tattered and I was not wearing shoes, instead, black, long claws took the place of my toes. I was a straight out monster. I let out a roar befor

e charging him and devouring his flesh as he lay there dying
, screaming. I woke up from that dream with a splitting headach
e. I felt dehydrated and drained of energy, but I couldn't go ba
ck to sleep. Instead, I told Izzy about it. She listened to my story
but was not exactly thrilled to hear that she was in it. I kind of wa
nted to let that detail out, but I can't seem to keep things from he
r. She sang to me and rubbed my head until I passed back out.
When I woke back up, she was packing things into the car. Sh
e said we needed to get on the road. She has an idea to head o
ut west, towards Oregon to see if any of her family out there is st
ill alive. They live on the outskirts of Portland. I didn't argue wit
h her about it, though I have a suspicion that they're not still aliv
e, and if they are, I don't foresee them accepting a thing like me.
I guess we'll see.

67.

My body hurts. My whole body. My skin feels like it's going to rip
open, and my bones hurt like they're breaking. I haven't felt a w
hole lot of pain, other than my headaches lately. Even when I go
t shot, it didn't really hurt. My mouth no longer tastes like rot an
y more. Kind of tastes normal again. Either I'm getting used to th
e taste, or it's getting better. I at least have saliva again. For a w
hile, I was always dry mouthed no matter how much liquid I co
nsumed. Speaking of my gunshot wound, it's completely healed
up. Not even a scar. I was shot a couple of days ago, now, nothi
ng. My fingertips and nails are extremely tender, as are my gum
s, mainly where they meet the teeth. I've been taking pills to hel

p, but I end up puking them up, and it doesn't seem to help any
ways. I want to drink some of the whisky I took from the house I
was holding up in, but Izzy won't let me. She says she needs m
e to be alert in case there's trouble. I feel like a damn child.

68.

We've been driving for hours, only stopping for bathroom breaks
, and gas. I am assuming that gas is going to become a hard thi
ng to come by as the months go on since we're not the only surv
ivors in this country. As we drive, it's not hard for my mind to
drift and think about all sorts of shit. I wonder what is happenin
g in other countries. Did this disease spread to places like Japan
? China? Germany? I wonder what they're doing to deal with it.
From what I have seen so far as we travel, the US really didn't
have time to react. I wonder what really caused this. It's not like
the zombie movies or television shows where a cast of attractive
people hole up in a local mall and all end up dying in some heroi
c fashion. It's not like the show where people were just turning
right after they died and the zombies were all slow and easily
dispatched. These ones are unpredictable. Some of them are fa
st, others are slow. They don't seem to get tired, or notice when
they're hurt. They keep coming until they're dead, or they get dis
tracted. None of them seem interested in me, I think they sense
me as one of them. I have seen them carry and use weapons,
crudely, but they still used them. Then there's the whole ran
dom effect with their bites. Just because you got bit, doesn't me
an you turn. Sometimes, other things happen. Take my infection

for example. I am constantly changing. Though, I am definitely, visibly infected, I am also, still intelligent, cognitive. I still feel thin gs like pain, sadness, anger.... My friend is still there, so I am sti ll mentally unstable, so at least that has not changed lol! But, the re is just this feeling of uncertainty that doesn't go away. It's with you like an unwelcomed houseguest. It is with you even when y ou find a "Safe" place to rest. The people in all of the communes that we have found so far, are always paranoid of other people o utside of the group, they're always concerned with stockpiling re sources, and are unwilling to share. The longer that we manage to survive, the less "good" people we seem to find. We're going t o be stopping for the night here in a few minutes. So, it's bye for now.

69.

We found an old video store in the middle of nowhere. It looks li ke it was closed before everything went to shit. It has old VHS tapes, some DVDs, and even the older gaming consoles. If ther e was any electricity, I would hook up the old systems and play some games! But no power.... I am however grabbing what I can, who knows, there may be another place with power eventu ally. We're going to crash out for the night and then head out in the morning.

70.

I was awakened by Izzy screaming. I thought that a zombie had gotten in, but it was a spider. I had almost forgotten she is still a child. With all that's happened, it's hard to consider anyone big enough to defend themselves as a child, but she is. It's not like I see her as an adult, but she isn't a child to me. She acts like an adult, she kills like an adult, she's an adult to me. I don't know w hat I would do if she really left me on my own. Before this transf ormation, I was fine with being alone, but now, I feel like she's th e one helping me stay as human as I can. I'm probably not maki ng sense, but nothing in this world does anymore. I'm tired, so I'm going back to sleep. "I fucking hate spiders!" She says. LOL

71.

We woke up. She ate some of the food we had been stockpiling, I of course didn't eat anything. It's pretty inconvenient to have a diet such as mine, especially when me getting something to eat i s so horrendous to witness. I am still trying to figure out a way to maybe find a less disturbing thing to do for my hunger, but th e only thing I can eat without puking, or being in excruciating pai n, is zombie flesh. This sucks, and I'm hungry. I would serio usly give my left eye for a fucking pizza. Not that I can keep it do wn. I just want to be at least normal again. But I don't think there is a cure for what is wrong with me. Another thing that bothers m e is, what if, I survive until the end of all of this? What if, these z ombies, being my food, are all killed off? What do I do then? Other than maybe, and I mean MAYBE, starve to death? I hate having all of these questions, which may not be answered until the actually time comes. So far, it doesn't seem that I can die conventionally. I'm not about to put a gun to my head just yet, but, what if that doesn't kill me? Then what? I don't want to live like this forever. There has to be an end eventually, right? Well, we're leaving. TTYL

72.

So, we're on the outskirts of Portland now. She's getting more and more excited. I am doing my best to act excited as well, though I highly doubt we're going to find anything different than we have seen the rest of the trip out here. I remember when I used to go on trips with my grandparents and how I would just sit there for hours imagining what it was going to be like when we got to where we were going. I was never correct. It was almost always a disappointment with the exception of the few times it happened to be an amusement park of some sort that we were going to. I may not have been a normal kid by definition, but I really did enjoy the thrill of roller coasters and the food they sold at these places. Never have I had hotdogs that tasted quite as good as the ones they sold there. I think I actually miss being a kid once in a while. I was fucked up, but being a kid was so much simpler than the shit that we have to deal with as adults, especially in my life. I am kind of appreciative of the apocalypse thing happening because I was not good at being an adult. I was awkward, unable to function within the rules of society, and I was thoroughly unhappy. At least now I have a purpose in this world. I keep Izzy safe, and I eat zombies. I guess it could be worse.

73.

We are now in Portland. The weirdest thing about this place so far is that there are no zombies or people that we're seeing. It is amazingly clean, and there is nobody to be seen anywhere. All of the power works, the traffic signals still work, and so do the pumps at the gas stations. It's as if this place was cleaned up, and then left by everyone and everything that lived there. Maybe they're all hiding in these skyscrapers, but it really looks like there's nobody here. We got gas, and other provisions while we were there, and then we left for her, I guess cousin's house. Her cousin is, or should I say, was, a programmer for some video game company that made controversial and very violent content. I wasn't really into video games with the exception of the old retro ones. I like the classics, what can I say? I guess we're here now. Let's see if there is anyone still alive here.

74.

The gate to the driveway was chained shut, so we had to jump over the fence. I suggested we cut the chains with the bolt cutter, but she insisted that we at least make sure it's a safe place to stay before we commit to bringing our vehicle all the way up to the house. I can't say I disagreed. We also were unable to see the house from the gate, so we really weren't sure what we were goin g to be getting ourselves into. It seemed like about a mile walk b efore we finally saw it. The place was huge. The grass was obvi ously kept well, though I am confused as to how they would cut i t without paying attention to themselves. I'm sure there's a meth od to the madness, but that doesn't seem like an important thing at the moment. We got to the beginning of the sidewalk when w e were suddenly under fire. Someone on the roof I guess was fir ing warning shots, at least that's what the girl on the roof said. S he told us not to move and we wouldn't get shot. Right after that, an older male came walking out of the house and walked up to u s. He instantly recognized Izzy and gave her a big hug. The mo ment he looked at me, he motioned to the person on the roof, an d everything went black. I woke up in a hole in the ground, surro unded by dead zombies. I guess they had a mass grave for anyt hing dead that got through their gates. My head hurt so bad I co uldn't completely make out the sound of Izzy yelling at her cousi n over shooting me. I could make out words like, "asshole" "fuck er" and something about not shooting her pet. I guess I'm her pe t. That's weird. Whatever. I crawled out of the pit, it took a lot of effort, but I got out and walked towards the sound of their conver sation. I was then tackled to the ground by the female from the r ooftop and dragged into the basement. She tied me up and left me there for about what I thought was an hour. I could still hear t hem arguing upstairs as to what to do with me. Izzy was obvious ly not OK with what they had planned. Something about "The fu cking thing won't die, we need to chop it into tiny pieces, and the n burn those pieces." I was not OK with that shit either. I started

yelling at the top of my lungs to let me go. Nobody seemed to no
tice I was yelling. I got tired of waiting to get chopped up and de
cided to try to get out of the ropes and chair I was tied to. That w
ent OK, I guess. I fell over and had to struggle for a bit before th
e ropes got loose enough to get my hands free. I fucked up the
skin on my hands pretty good. I guess it's a good thing I don't bl
eed, still getting used to it. I finally got loose and went to a mirror
they had above a utility sink. My head hurt like shit and I was wa
nting to see what that did. As I assumed, she shot me in the fuc
king head. Awesome. I guess that doesn't kill me either. There
was just a hole. I could see through it. I felt the back of my head
and it seems that it's at least closing back up. I guess I have so
me slow sort of regeneration going on. I can't really complain th
ough it does put a damper on my thoughts of what to do when th
e whole zombie thing is over. I walked up the stairs to the door a
nd knocked. The conversation they were having then stopped a
nd they opened the door. Izzy was standing in front of me and w
ouldn't let her cousin and what I assumed was his girlfriend near
me. She told them to leave me alone or we were going to get ba
ck in our truck and go. She also told them she would have me kil
l them on the way out. I wasn't really wanting to do that, but I wo
uld have if she told me to. I guess I am her pet. They finally calm
ed down and let me get a change of clothes and told me to go g
et a shower. "You smell like week old dog shit" the woman said.
She didn't tell me her name at that moment. I guess she didn't f
eel it was important for me to know. Whatever. I'm going to go g
et my shower. TTYL.

75.

As luck would have it, the shower apparently did nothing to help my smell, if anything it made it worse. I can't personally smell m yself so I'm ok with it, Izzy never complains, maybe she went no se blind? Either way, the same woman that decided to tell me h ow I smell in case I was unaware, said I still smell like smashed assholes. I am super not impressed by her lack of funny insults based off how the person smells. Fucking amateur.

76.

Izzy and her relatives I guess didn't see eye to eye, so we left e arly in the morning. She had me go out to the truck to wait and s he grabbed all the food and supplies she could before anyone w as any the wiser and we took off. During the drive in no direction , we made a pit stop at a lone gas station to see if there was fuel for the truck. There was! There was enough to fill the truck, and the tanks in the back. Once I loaded all the gas cans up, which didn't take any effort at all to do, I thought that was weird. Normally movement and carrying things has been difficult since I assume my body is desiccating and that's going to put a damper on moving, but not anymore. Izzy wants to camp out here before we decide what we're going to do next.

77.

I was awakened by a scream and bolted out the gas station door towards the screaming.

Right as soon as I heard it, I knew it was Izzy. She's got a bad habit of wandering off on her own. I get that she's tough, but this situation right here, is what I'm talking about when I gripe at her about it. Anyways, I was running towards her, but instead, I ran right into a bear trap. It seems her cousins followed us and had some plans for me. I took out three of them before I was again blasted in the head by another fucking bullet the ground and incapacitated. I was taken in the back of the truck, and I could hear Izzy screaming at them to let us go, they were of course not listening. After a long drive that seemed to go on forever, we pulled up to what sounded like one of those security gates with wheels. Someone spoke from a metal shack and let them continue to drive. We pulled up to a building and the back of the truck was slammed open, there were bright lights making it hard to see, and then they dragged me out of the truck dumped me into a dank cell, with bars on the windows and there was a concrete slab for a b

ed. They kept it dark until they were going to come get me, and t
hey used more of the lights to keep me disoriented. We had to b
e there something like maybe 17 days, I lost count. They made
me their Guinee pig for whatever the fuck they were testing. I kn
ow that some of it did something to me. But no matter what it did
, I could look forward to being subjected to more disorienting shit
right after. I wasn’t given time to rest, they seemed to be workin
g in shifts, looking for a way to kill me. I just kept growing back.
And then one of those days, to their horrified surprise, some of t
he chunks they carved off of me started to move and crawl towa
rds them. They of course panicked and opened fire, which pisse
d the little gross shits off, which led to a bunch of face hugging,
screaming in terror, and soon, silence. I could hear a distant shu
ffling from in the further reaches of

the room my cell was in, and it was getting closer by the second
. A single body part came inching back to me, and I was excited
to have some help getting free, but, to my surprise and dismay, i
t was my dick... Yes, my penis. It crawled up my body and acros
s my face, and then it got to the chains where it seemed to die,
dissolve, or something gross, and then the chains melted away i
n a pool of black goop. I was free. Nobody will ever believe this
part happened but fuck them. Oh, and the rest of the parts did th
e same thing, but to the people's faces, throats, there wasn’t mu

ch left of them. I could tell there used to be a body there, but that's because I recognized that nightmare fuel right away. Once I was free, I knew I needed to go find where those fucks took Izzy to. I didn't see any of them or hear anything from the point I was thrown into that cell. FUCK. I need to find her.

78.

I wasn't able to find her. I fear that she's lost to me. I searched for days, weeks, I dunno, backtracking all the way to where her cousins lived. I could see that they took off from this place in a hurry, and the coffee pot was still on, boiling the coffee that was left in it to a thick, goopy mess. I assumed this was because the house didn't burn down. What were we warned about growing up? "You'll burn the fucking house down!!" Everyone would freak out about things like this. Anyways, there were too many things strewn about the house. Although, I did note that there were a lot of supplies left, then there was the smell. Something smelled good. Smelled so good I could not stop salivating. Like fresh cherry pies cooling on the counter. Just strong and inviting. The next thing I remember, I was in a room in the house I wasn't familiar with. It was fancy, like a ballroom fancy... And there were people everywhere. I was normal, and dressed nicely. I was being greeted by everyone I passed by. I finally got up to the line for the food, and I could see Izzy no more than six feet from me. But when I got up to her, someone punched me in the back of the head and I turned around, ready to fight, but instead, I was snapped out of the trance I was in and could see that her cousins were more than a live and Izzy was there standing there in front of me, looking shocked, as if she'd seen a ghost. When I looked down, I saw that I had torn her heart out of her chest. And the banquet I was getting ready to chow down on was their relatives they didn't have the heart to kill off, so they left them in there.

I fell to the floor, to my knees. Her family was attacking me, but I wasn't being hurt. They were muffled and I couldn't make out what they were screaming, but they were hitting me and crying, I was crying, holding Izzy in my arms, apologizing to her as she gasped for breath, until she didn't. She went limp and was with us no more. Wiping the tears from my eyes, I stood up, shrugging her very reasonably upset family members off of me and walked out the door. I never looked back. And then I was alone again. Now, I'm alone.

79.

I am still trying to understand why this happened. I have never felt bad about killing people. I had not had feelings of remorse, or regret over something like this before. I wasn't sad when I killed my "best friend". Why was this different? Why was I so depressed by it? She was a kid that I barely knew from before the zombie apocalypse happened, and I only knew who she was because I killed her fucking disgusting stepdad. Thinking about the bastard makes my teeth grind with rage. I needed to go eat. So, I went hunting and gorged on dead flesh until I couldn't eat any more and then promptly passed out in a field full of dead zombies.

80.

I woke up the next morning and I noticed something right away wasn't right. My body is fully healed, and I seem to be back to normal, as in I look human. The thing is, yesterday I was a monster laying in a field covered in rotting flesh, and now I look normal. Actually, I look better than normal. I feel ALIVE! I can feel, but I can't seem to feel pain where before I wasn't feeling anything. I walked into a trap someone set up in a rest stop lobby, it was a shotgun rigged door. Funny enough, the pellets didn't even break the skin, but it made a mess of my shirt, or should I say it fucking Swiss cheesed it! Food is still a no go for me. As soon as I put it in my mouth, it's like the food broke down and decomposed as soon as it hit saliva. I now realize that's exactly what's happening. As I was spitting out the disgusting mass of mold and rot, I noticed that the ground was smoking or steaming? Not really sure to be honest. But either way, the ground was melting away in the spot that I spit my food out on. It's not acid, it's more like necrosis. It doesn't burn away things, it rots them. I've also noticed I have black gums, and two rows of teeth when I eat. It's a row of regular looking teeth and gums, but the second I go to eat, the second row comes out and my gums turn black. The second row of teeth look like wet obsidian and they're sharp pointed. Another thing is that my fingertips turned black as if I dipped them in ink

, but that's all I noticed other than they were hard to touch at that time. I have a feeling this is going to be a week or more of new e xperiences... Sarcasm.

81.

I had a nightmare again; this time it was Izzy I killed as my first. She was my age at the time, and I killed her in those woods and got the wolves to eat her. My mother switched places with my fa ther in my dream as well. So, my mom did all the killing and he s tood there smiling like nothing was wrong while he bled out. Did n't even react to being cut. Just grinning. Then there was fire. M y grandfather in his fucking station wagon screaming at me to let him out, and then bursting into flames along with the rest of the car. My grandmother took pills to die.

Each of these events took place and ended up in a display case commemorating those events. I walked away from her death sc ene to notice I was in a cavernous museum. I had to get out of t here, so I walked out of the exit only to find that I was walking rig ht back into that same museum. I couldn't leave. It's then that I woke up. I sat up from laying down and sitting in front of me, Izz

y.

It seems that I now have a new imaginary friend. Ok then. I'm go ing with it.

82.

I suspect Izzy isn't actually her. She's erratic and seems to be ar guing with herself a lot. Of course, I have tried to check on her, but that never goes well. Last time I tried to ask her what was go ing on, she just stood up and pointed at me, and then she let out this crazy scream. It was loud enough to make my ears feel a pr essure change, I got a nosebleed, and threw up. I got up and ch arged her to stop it, but that's when I remembered, she's not rea lly there, and this is all in my head. I remembered this very impo rtant detail when I got up from tackling a garbage can. Of course , I was also being taunted by her laughing and pointing at me. S eemingly everywhere I looked, I saw her, laughing, pointing. It w as more than I could handle, and I passed out. I am really annoy ed that I'm no longer like I was before. I didn't care about being clean, or even get bothered by my friend. She's so much worse. She's literally fucking staring at me from the dark corner of the g arage as I'm writing this. She's always there and she's having a great time. I haven't gotten anything done because I'm frustrate d and annoyed. Fuck.

Chapter 13 – WTF

83.

I was awakened at who the fuck cares? Early, to the sound of grunting and cussing. I sat up to see, and to my surprise, Izzy had found some way to lure my friend out and now had him pinned to the ground. She looked at me and smiled, he looked over at me, and she used that distraction to drive a screwdriver into the side of his head. She left it there, his eyes still affixed on mine. I really didn't know how to react. It wasn't shocking to see someone die that doesn't even exist; it was shocking to see that she managed to kill him. I couldn't feel his shitty presence anymore and I was left feeling lighter.

"Jesus fucking Christ, Izzy! How did you fucking do that?!" I yelled, out loud, because, at this point, I no longer treat this like it's not real, because it is to me, and who is there to stop me?

"I don't know dude, I'm *your* imaginary friend, so maybe ask yourself?" Izzy bellows, sounding extremely annoyed and outright exhausted.

I told her I was at least really glad to be rid of that other friend, even though she was imaginary. I think the main reason she exist s, and he was killed off by her, was my feeling of guilt for her death. And since she's one of the only people that knew who and what I was before all this shit went down, I guess this is the result.

84.

This morning, we were on the road, meaning, I was on the road, talking to myself, when I happened to be at an old church. It was burned for the most part but had obviously been used as shelter at some point since the shit went down. In this church, I found a very interesting book in someone's pack. It's a bible, but all of the pages but a couple have been burned out. There is an entry in ink, then blood, it reads:

"THE NEW TESTAMENT OF JESUS CHRIST – 2025AD

See, that I am the son of God, and you are being judged by us. You failed to heed the warnings in the books written for you to understand in every language. You chose not to yield to serve our one true God, and therefore, you shall parish, your flesh burned, your spirit cleansed, and you will be placed in the eternal flames of Hell!

For you have all been fooled! This God that was described in the books made available by the "Men of God" has been misrepresented. For the God in this book has been truly, Lucifer himself! All of "God's Men" have been pedophiles, rapists, gluttonous, lusting for the flesh of the innocent. In all of the secret rituals, cha nting, in all of the holy places, idolatry, lust, sin, forgiveness! It's all lies people! I, Jesus, am here to help you all reach the Real God! But you have to find me here, in all of this! I can't tell you w here I will be by the time you read this, but, I am out there, I ass ure you, and as long as you live, as do I. I will be here until the l ast human is dead, or humanity is safe once again. FIND ME, n o matter your condition, your sins, your ailments, I will help you. "

I put the book into my bag and decided to walk for a few miles b efore getting near the road that the church was on, I felt somethi ng was waiting for a poor unfortunate person, to stumble into the trap they had set. I was right. At the three-mile mark, I saw a va n, and a couple tents set up. There were three people standing outside of a large, military style tent, and there were two other, s maller tents behind the big one. I could hear conversations of w here to go next. So, I'm going to investigate this place further an d see what these people are doing.

85.

I got caught, of course, and they tortured me long enough to real ize that I was definitely not human anymore, and that of course I ed right to their trying to kill me... Well, that didn't go well for the m. They held me in a cage for fucking what seemed like an eter nity. I was starved for YEARS... I saw things during the solitary c onfinement, starvation, in complete darkness in the deepest part of their compound that they then barricaded, bricked, and forgot about. My mind was broken to the point where I was hallucinating and lucid dreaming at the same time. Harder than the heroes' dose of LCD and so spiritually profound that you come out permanently different. So much dreamless sleep, I killed my imaginary friend and ate her to sustain myself, to obviously no satiation. I was broken down and abandoned. I don't know how long I was in captivity, but when they couldn't kill me, then, they decided to bury me and forget I exist. I didn't really know what was going on at the time that enough damage had been done to get myself out of that hell, but there was an explosion overtop. Like a nuclear one. It cracked the foundation of the building I was in, and when I dug my way to the surface, there was just disintegrated remains of humanity. Not a lot of people survived this at all. But I am seemingly immune to radiation, and there are now plenty of undead fuckers to eat, so at least I won't be hungry…I will do what I can to help any survivors I find, but I fear most will be like me, a wolf in sheep's clothing, an apex predator with one purpose. To feed. This new world is fucked up.

86.

Let's talk about what happened to me in that church….

Firstly, I fucking HATE religion. I think it's all disgusting. Secondly, I HATE evangelists, and especially ones that pray on the people around them with a false image of being a good person. These people were sick. But of course, when you think about it, wouldn't everyone alive at this point be pretty fucked up? Think abou

t it. What have we all had to do to survive this thing? Nobody se
ems to really know what happened. I think I know, but to be hon
est, I am not entirely sold. I think the government did this, or the
elites, that cunt in the World Economic Forum? Maybe that billio
naire that was buying up all the farmland and introducing lab gro
wn meats into the market? That one is fucked up because the fo
od industry, the CDC, the WEF, and major computer software c
ompanies were all in on that. They didn't even have to tell us in t
he grocery store that the meat we're buying wasn't naturally bor
n, but lab grown meat. They definitely didn't tell us about the bull
shit that the Vatican was on, or that the government of the world
decided all to sign a treaty to never allow researchers full acces
s to places like the south pole???? Fucking whatever! The world
ended because a dickhead elite had the idea to cause a global p
andemic, and the dumb fucks thought they could hide in their bu
nkers while things played out. Well, jokes on them, because we'
re out here going on 20 fucking years! I have seen zombies that
look like normal people, me included. I have abilities that don't
make any sense in any scientific manner. I should not be able to
consume dead flesh, and dead flesh ONLY. Nothing else sustai
ns my hunger, and even better, this diet has made me stronger,
has seemingly corrected my mental problems from before the e
nd happened. I no longer have hallucinations of my "Friend" as I
called it. As I said in my last entry, I ate her... It was he, and the
n her, and then no more. I gained nothing on a nutritional level fr
om consuming my companion, but I gained my independence fr
om an entity I made up in my head. I was freed. Every time I eat

undead flesh, I am filled with absolute happiness that can only b e described by the yogis as "Shangri la" or complete nirvana. I a m at peace with the universe and whole as a being of heightene d consciousness though externally to onlookers, it would be des cribed as the "single most disgusting and foul abomination to Go d, and an absolute afront to the holy fucking church."

The last words of the priest that sealed my fate, and their own.

All these have come to pass and still, I find some good people e xisting. Some kind, some not, some smart, some very deceitful and sick, people too. The bunkers where the elites were braggin g, they had, were overtaken and then repurposed after "Eat the Rich" became something really, well… Real... There is nothing l eft to stop humanity from evolving, and it's all thanks to the fuck ers in some country I wouldn't go to if they paid me. And I mean, those people were really sick. I am going to go on adventures to places we weren't allowed to go. Nothing can stop me from bein g alive, and every time I eat, I only get stronger and better, so let 's see them stop me, not that there's anything to see here!! Noth ing at all...

87.

Goodbye.

It's been fun, but I am like I said in the last entry, going on an ad venture. I won't be sharing what I find here, I leave that shit to y ou, fucking weird ass person reading the lamentations of a mad man. Love you, be nice to each other, there's worse shit out ther e, like, well.... Me... Either way, Epstein didn't kill himself, Disne y was owned by the British Empire, so was the US, the CIA was indeed doing stuff to everyone, there were "mud flood" catastrop hes, genetically cloned orphans being delivered to doorstep of el ites, whole continents were lied about and the real chosen land of the biblical people was in America and Africa, this was attribut ed to the colonialist and Asian indigenous peoples of America w anting to remove a melanin rich indigenous people from their rig htful home and promised land, then further desecrating the land by putting satanic and demonic imagery and worship all over the country, basing the very education system entrusted with our chi ldren with indoctrinated bullshit history, and all sort of other lies were found to be TRUTHS. Man, he faces of people when they saw the original depictions of Jesus. Not that his name was real, or that the bible was right. Because again, that was based on bu llshit mostly too. God isn't external, nor does god need worship. We are Gods. As are all living things, including plants, animals, and yes, unfortunately, everyone else. God is not special and do esn't want to be. It just wants us to evolve so that someday, we may actually speak face to face. That is found through a conscio usness shift that everyone that has survived all of the events of t he past 20 something years. We who survive, have been given gifts, abilities, and insight. My abilities have yet to show much li mit past what I can manifest. The better I am at focusing on wha t I want to do, the better the result. My body morphs and change s to what I am doing at the time. But I always end up looking like a normal dickhead in the end. So, it's got its limits, I guess. Or I would look like, I don't know, not this ugly motherfucker lol!

Take care of yourselves out there, I hope we can all make some thing better of this horrible state of fuckery. --J

Made in the USA
Columbia, SC
12 March 2024

911f3421-0266-4e5a-80e4-ff48dafd3284R02